Advanced Praise for *She Nailed a Stake Through His Head*

This book takes the Bible back from those right-wing fascists who
want to rewrite it as a tedious book of loving and caring. These are
stories as bawdy and lustful and horrifying as the original Good
Book - wild sex, savage violence, horrific curses...and, of course,
vampires.

> - Matthue Roth, author of *Never Mind the Goldbergs* and
> *Candy in Action*

You don't need to be Jewish or Christian to appreciate *She Nailed a
Stake Through His Head: Tales of Biblical Terror*. Still, you may find
yourself groping for a religious icon for protection given the
unholy places these weird tales will take you.

Meandering between desert sands and skyscrapers, between past,
present and alternate timelines, *She Nailed a Stake Through His Head*
is a gallery of horrors inspired by the most nightmarish images of
Near Eastern cultures. There are wild-eyed, drug-crazed prophets,
witches drawing the dead from the depths of the Underworld,
sacred prostitutes, an English Delilah trapped in a house falling
down around her, epic beheadings and a living tomb in the foul
and slimy body of a whale.

Regardless of religion (or lack thereof), lovers of speculative
fiction will swallow up these provocative stories.

> - Erin O'Riordan, author of *Beltane* and *Midsummer Night*

"Lyrical, horrifying, beautiful and thought provoking, *She Nailed a
Stake Through His Head* is a sharp read and well worth your time
whether or not you are familiar with the biblical tales the stories
reference."

> - Jennifer Brozek, winner of the 2009 Australian Shadows
> Award for edited publication

Sex, death, passion and blood - all the best secrets of the so-called "Good Book." Give a copy to the holy roller on your block...then stand back and watch his head explode!
- SatyrPhil Brucato, *Witches & Pagans Magazine*

Who knew the bible contained chillers? It's widely acknowledged that the bible is filled to the brim with tales of romance, heroism, violence, and mysticism. *She Nailed a Stake through his Head: Tales of Biblical Terror* shines a spotlight on the suspense stories lingering in biblical shadows. If you know your bible, then the territory is familiar but I doubt if you've ever considered the landscape from this perspective before. Consider, for example, what actually caused the deaths of Ruth's husband, brother-in-law and father-in-law? Do crucifixes really drive vampires away? *She Nailed a Stake through His Head* contains genuine tales of horror plus much food for thought. An excellent and diverse collection of stories, special highlights include Gerri Leen's "Whither Thou Goest" and "Last Respects" by D.K. Thompson.
- Judika Illes, author of *The Encyclopedia of Spirits, The Encyclopedia of 5000 Spells* and *The Weiser Field Guide to Witches*

Variety, interpretation, Bible stories with a bite where half the fun is in figuring out which part of Scripture provided the source!
- James S. Dorr, author *Darker Loves: Tales of Mystery* and *Regret*

She Nailed a Stake Through His Head:
Tales of Biblical Terror

Edited by Tim Lieder

Dybbuk Press
New York, NY
October 2010

Printed in New York

ISBN: 0-9766546-7-9
13-number ISBN: 978-0-9766546-7-4
Library of Congress Control Number: 2010924983

Copyright History
"Swallowed!" © 2005 Stephen M. Wilson, originally appeared in *Wicked Karnival*
"Babylon's Burning" © 2010 Daniel Kaysen, originally appeared in *Black Static*, Feb-March 2010 issue.
"Last Respects" © 2007 Dave Thompson, originally appeared in *Pseudopod*.
"Whither Thou Goest" © 2010 Gerri Leen
"Jawbone of an Ass" © 2010 Lyda Morehouse
"Judgment at Naioth" © 2010 Elissa Malcohn
"Judith & Holofernes" © 2010 Romie Stott
"As if Favorites of their God" © 2010 Christi Krug
"Psalm of the Second Body" © 2005 Catherynne M. Valente, originally appeared in *PEN Book of Voices*, edited by Michael Butscher
Introduction © 2010 Tim Lieder

Cover designed by Tim Lieder

Cover painting is *Jael and Sisera* by Jacopo Amigoni

Dedicated to Dr. Dassie Naiman

Great friend, Torah enthusiast and the strangest woman I've ever met. This book would not have been possible without her encouragement.

Table of Contents

Introduction

Blame Joseph Heller. Many bad influences led to this anthology, but Joseph Heller wrote *God Knows*, which I read after taking a rather mind-blowing class entitled *The Bible: Wisdom, Poetry and Apocalyptic*. When you're a college student, mind-blowing religious books are standard, but you expect to get your mind blown by Starhawk, Tom Robbins, Robert Anton Wilson and the Maharishi. You don't expect to find much in a text that you've already dismissed as patriarchal, hierarchal, racist and the basis for every evil in the world from genocide to Christian rock. After writing my final paper comparing the Book of Koheleth (Ecclesiastes) to the Tao Teh Ching, I was eager for more and Heller filled the niche.

God Knows depicts King David with borsht belt comedian pathos. He's complaining about Michal. He's trying to shtup Bathsheba one last time. He's very defensive when it comes to his relationship with Jonathan. He dismisses Samson as a messhuggah out to put his putz into as many shiksas as possible (Mad Magazine had conditioned me for the equation "Yiddish=Hilarity" so this bit had me laughing for days. I was also under a lot of stress.) And like Heller's *Catch-22*, the humor serves to barely conceal the tragic nature of the tale. Ultimately, Heller's David is a sad and lonely man whose life's work has isolated him from all loved ones. His only true father figure tried to kill him. His wives despise him and his best general killed his favorite son. In the final page, David is left uncertain whether any of it was worth the sacrifice.

When I read the Book of Samuel, I was pleasantly surprised to find Heller's mixture of low humor and high tragedy consistent with the original. The story of David has all the rape, patricide, fratricide, betrayal and civil war that you're ever going to want in an epic - but also a terrible beauty and a sense of joy that cannot be mitigated even in the most tragic moments. Joseph Heller not only introduced me to the concept of the Bible as literature, but also put his own unique stamp on a story that I only thought I knew. Since then, I've had a particular appreciation for Biblical literature.

Sadly, much of the modern fare relies on children's stories and apocalyptic screeching. Where once stood *Paradise Lost* now resides *Left Behind*. For every intelligent Bible series like NBC's short lived *Kings*, there are dozens of uninspired "Biblical Epics" featuring actors droning in potato sacks and Richard Gere disco dancing in a diaper.

With this anthology, I hope to fill that void and honor the writers who have used Biblical themes brilliantly without resorting to puerile themes. Out of the nine stories, six are based on Tanakh (also known as The Old Testament), one is New Testament, one is from Apocrypha and one is a meditation on the Epic of Gilgamesh. Within that framework, the stories embrace many styles including alternate history, experimental, Lovecraftian terror, midrash and historical romance.

This is only a small sampling of the vast wealth of literary possibilities.

For further discussion of the Bible's literary themes, I'd recommend Robert Alter's pair of books, *The Art of Biblical Poetry* and *The Art of Biblical Prose* as well as Rabbi Hayyim Angel's *Through an Opaque Lens*. There are also several excellent graphic novels dealing with Biblical themes including *The Cartoon History of the Universe* by Larry Gonick and Robert Crumb's *Genesis*. If you can find a copy of *Outrageous Tales from the Old Testament*, buy it. Neil Gaiman contributed and it's out of print, so it might be pricey. Of course, reading the Bible itself is recommended but try to find a decent translation. Even though King James is considered the most beautiful version, there are other fine translations including the Jewish Publication Society's translation and Everett Fox's *The Five Books of Moses* which preserves the original poetic tropes.

Whither Thou Goest
By Gerri Leen

In the stories of those who survive, I am a heroine. In the stories of my own people, those of us descended from Lot's daughter, from her incestuous union with her own father, I am also a heroine. If two such noble peoples see me as such, who am I to complain?

They both love me because I endure. Because I survive. Because I cling with holy (or is it unholy) fervor to the woman who bore the man I sucked dry. Once she knew what I was, Naomi would have killed me if she could, but her life is forfeit if I should cease to draw breath. I saw to that when I said the ancient words, binding me to her, twining my very breath with hers.

"Wherever you go, I will go…"

Beautiful, aren't they, these words of power? Of control. Lot's daughters were forced to follow their father into the desert, their mother covering herself with salt for protection against the demon that had overtaken her husband - a demon who burned her in place, leaving only her salted, charred corpse. Lot's daughters, unnamed in the books of the survivors, but known to my people, learned to turn the words of servitude into words of angry potency after their father raped them. The survivors changed the story, turned the girls into the ones who sought their father to ensure their progeny's life, but we remember. Those of us who hold fast, who suck dry. Who never leave once we latch on.

"Wherever you lodge, I will lodge…"

None can rid themselves of us once we take hold. Not while we cling.

"Don't beg me to leave you, or to stop following you..."

Once there were words of rebuke, designed to claw my kind from the lives of the faithful. But they were lost long before I found Naomi, and her husband, and her sons. My sister Orpah and I flipped a coin, the hammered side meaning she would take hold and follow this woman to a new land. But the carved side fell instead, and it was up to me.

It hurt to say goodbye to my sister. Perhaps the only hurt I'd felt for a long time.

Naomi could tell.

"Look, your sister-in-law is going back to her people, and to her gods; follow her." My sister-in-truth did go back to our gods, and I pledged myself to Naomi's one god, the boundless skies crackling with delight at my heresy.

I was consecrated in blood years before. I belonged to the old ones. I would keep my husband's mother in a stranglehold, but not so tight that she ran out of air. For I spoke true when I said, "Where you die, I will die, and there will I be buried." I was tied to her as surely as she was to me. And I have a fear of being trapped underground. We were born in caves and we fled them as soon as we could, dancing under the stars, lying naked under the fierce winds of the desert, letting the blowing sand scour any remaining sanctity from us.

Naomi begged me to stay with Orpah. She wept. She bribed. She even tried to stab me in the night. Fortunately, I am a light sleeper. I cause nightmares; I do not have them.

In the end, she gave up. I called her hag, doomed one, lost lamb. It amused me to watch her become silent as we traveled together.

But near Bethlehem, when we stopped for water, I overheard her telling a stout young man who was watering his flock that I was a demon. He laughed at her, but later I caught him following us. I bade him join us, and he basked in the venomous warmth of my smile. I let him into our camp - let him into me - as I sucked him dry, and drained the vitality and goodness out of him. I left him a husk of a man on the road to Bethlehem. His seed died within me. He was not of Naomi's line; my womb rejected his offering.

Naomi wept bitter tears for him. She thought he looked like my husband, her son. I thought so too. I enjoyed the similarities.

"You are unnatural," she said as I stood in the creek and washed the last of him out of me.

"Oh, I exist in the natural world. I don't disappear in the light of day." Some of my kind did; they hunted only in the dark, drinking their victim's life away much faster, more directly through the blood. They lived long, the dark dwellers, not tied to their victims. But my kind lived our shorter lives in the open, and that made us stronger, more alive.

"You are heinous. A cursed thing. Nothing good lives in you."

She was right. Inside, if I let myself feel it, beat the remnants of the broken heart of Lot's girl, robbed of her mother, then of her innocence. Her pain passed through our line, diluted in most of the Moabites. But strong in some of us, those who learned how to turn pain into suffering - into slow, ingenious torture of the soul. We lived to break others; it was the only way we could survive, then later it was the only way we could thrive.

I thought Naomi a broken woman when we arrived in Bethlehem. But she stood before her old neighbors, telling the truth - if those who listened could have understood her words. She said, "Don't call me Naomi; call me Mara, for the Almighty has dealt very bitterly with me. I went out full, and the Lord had brought me home again empty. Why call me Naomi, seeing how the Lord has judged me, how the Almighty has afflicted me?"

None understood. None saw that I was the curse she spoke of. They saw only a young devoted woman. I hugged her as she finished her speech.

"I like it here," I said as I pulled her close and bit down on her neck, not breaking skin, but sucking hard enough to leave a bruise just behind her ear.

"Leave me," she said, and her voice seemed to shatter, as if her last hope had been here, in this place, with these people. Had she thought that her homeland could save her from me?

"I can never leave you. But I can add to our family." And I turned to look at her kinsman Boaz, a handsome, wealthy man who smiled with delight on both of us.

"No." Naomi's voice was little more than breath, warm across my face as she pulled me to face her. "Do what you will with me. But leave him alone."

"What you love, I will love."

She fell away from me with a cry, and I let her go. My eyes met Boaz's, and he was mine. Even if he didn't know it, even if his blood was not yet singing for me, I could feel the spark of attraction that would someday bind him.

I lowered my eyes, keeping them downcast as a young maiden should. I hurried after Naomi and did not look back. But if I had, Boaz would have been staring after me.

And now I make plans for him. He knows me only as the Moabite who followed her beloved mother-in-law home. "How do I win him?" I ask Naomi, when I find her in our new house, small and not very tidy. Where are all the riches of my father-in-law?

"I will not help you."

"This Boaz will care for us. He will spoil us and make us the envy of every woman in town." I do not relish sharing this with Naomi, but the binding works both ways. I cannot forsake her, not once the words have been spoken.

She will not answer.

"I will kill him if I cannot win him." I lean in, press my lips against hers and feel her shudder at my touch. "Shall I do that? Shall I kill him?"

She pulls away and I let her. Her lips are chapped where mine rested against them.

"You lack the humility to win him," she says.

"A challenge. I do love those."

To my surprise, she tells me of the old ways, the gleaning and the barley and corn I must gather. Her eyes gleam in a strange way when she speaks of water vessels that can only be touched with Boaz's permission; of the danger from following strange men in a field.

"You think they will harm me? You think they *can* harm me?"

"If you dishonor us, they will stone us both." She does not care anymore, the old witch. She may dishonor us herself if given half the chance.

I pull her to me, lips pressed again to hers, sucking in this time, pulling her strength, leaving just enough to let her get around the house but nothing more. She falls when I let her go and I do not help her up.

"They will not stone us, old woman."

I leave her and seek out Boaz's fields, keeping my head down, picking up the hatefully sharp gleaning, pieces

17

of grain that would not have been good enough for my horses back in the house where Orpah and I grew up.

I do not join in with the other girls; I go home to Naomi when it is time rather than sitting and laughing as they do. I do not talk to the young men. I understand that Boaz, who rides through the fields upon occasion, has told them to stay away from me.

I make sure the townsfolk see me helping Naomi, bringing a chair for her and putting it outside the front door when the sun goes down and the dust settles. She is weak, and she hasn't the energy to glare at me, but her hatred pulses between us.

"I will have him, hag. And then we will live in his fine house. And dine at his rich table. And I will suck the life from him just as I did your husband and sons." I lean in. "But not before he has given me a son."

"A son who is an abomination," she murmurs.

"Not until his lips fasten on my breast. His path is unclear until then." I lean back and stroke my belly as if life already grows in it. When my son nurses from me, I will feed him the pain of Lot's daughter, and he will grow strong in the memories. "Orpah has the sight, mother mine. She had a vision the day we left, told me that from my loins would come kings."

"We have no king here."

"Not yet." I grab her hand as I see Boaz approach. I can feel Naomi trying to muster energy to speak, and I suck hard on her essence until she grows too weak to talk.

"Kinswoman, you prosper?" Boaz crouches at her feet, and I watch him through my hair as I keep my face turned down. "And you, Ruth?"

"We are well fed, thanks to you."

"It is very little that I give you."

18

"It is more than we had." I lift my head, let him gaze on me. I know I am beautiful.

"I must go." He does not look eager to go.

I reach out, let my hand fall on his forearm, and read everything from the way his pulse races in the veins beneath my touch. He wants me. He will do anything for me. Except ask me outright. Except marry me. I am...

I am beneath him?

With a last smile, he walks away, calling out to those he passes.

"Ruth," Naomi says, her voice shaking in anger as much as exhaustion.

I grab her hand and give her back some of the energy I've stolen.

"What, old woman?"

"He was nothing when I left. My husband towered above him." Naomi's voice is brittle. "He gives us his leavings."

"Yes." I stroke her hand. "And a moment of his time."

I can feel a war inside her. It surprises me, but she's been burdened with me for so long as a second, hateful skin. Perhaps I am rubbing off on her?

"You want me to have him?"

She looks torn. Then she touches the faded robe she wears, and smiles wistfully. "I would like a glass of wine. Fine wine, like we had in Moab."

"Wouldn't we all." But I give her back a little more energy. This is interesting. "Myself, I'm getting tired of picking up grain."

"It is beneath you." Naomi meets my eyes with a look of hate, but one that seems devoid of its usual self righteousness. "But it is beneath me, too."

19

"And we are one, Mother." She normally hates it when I call her that, but she seems not to even notice it this time. As I help her inside, I ask, "Surely, there is a way to get what we deserve?"

"An old ritual. But one that cannot be denied."

"Tell me."

She does, her voice faltering as she details what I must do, so I fill her with energy again. "Hide among the grain," she says. "Wait until Boaz drinks with the men and falls asleep on the threshing floor, then lie at his feet and let him wake to find you there."

It reeks of the stories Naomi's people tell of Lot's daughters. Get a man drunk, have your way with him. All to get an heir. A son. A life beyond this one.

But to get a king, I will do it. Naomi looks at me as I bathe; she doesn't avert her eyes as she so often does.

"What?" I ask.

"You do not look evil." She leans in. "But you are. Your evil corrupts like rot on bread."

"I think I'm a bit more subtle." I laugh as I wind the finest cloth we have around me. And then I kiss her, not draining her this time, for once feeling she is indeed my mother, and she lets me hold her, doesn't pull from my lips. "We will live better than this."

Naomi shudders as I pull away, her hands clutching at me, as if she can keep me from Boaz.

"He is a good man."

I wait. I want to see her fall. I want to see her give in to our power. But she mutters to herself, an ancient prayer to her God. I feel a different power grow around her, a power that pushes me out of her a little.

But only a little.

"Wish me luck," I say as I go to find Boaz.

The wait is boring, the sound of men laughing and drinking tedious. I send my spirit casting through the sky, into the far reaches of this land, seeking out any who are like me. Here and there I find them. The dark ones. The cursed ones. And those just awakening to their power.

I come back to my body when I hear Boaz settling down in the grain. I crawl to his side and sit watching him. Then I put my fingers on his lips; let them trail down his chin, his neck, his chest, stopping when I reach his waist. I can feel his energy, such vitality. He will give me a strong son.

With that thought in my heart, I lie at his feet and wait. He snores. He rolls. He talks in his sleep. The sun is nearly up and he has still not stirred. I grab a sharp blade of grain, poke it into his foot, and then let it fall as he finally wakes.

"Who's there?" His heart is beating; I can feel his fear.

I sit up as if confused from sleep. "I am Ruth, your handmaid." My hand steals to his calf, grips it lightly. "Claim me, for you are my family."

He does not look happy. I drag lightly at his essence, pulling what I need into me. He is familiar, enough like Naomi that I can twine myself into him the same way I do her.

"I am yours," I say.

What I mean, of course, is that he is mine.

Sweat beads on his forehead as he makes plans for our future. I feel his vitality flowing into me, and from far off, I can tell that Naomi is feeling it too.

I leave him, secure in the knowledge that he will do as he must to have me. In time, ritual challenges are given and won. Naomi and I are moved into his fine house. I take him to bed, knowing Naomi can feel the edge of our passion.

When I check on her in the morning, she looks sick.

"Will it be like this always?"

"He is your blood. We are all one."

She holds a knife over a loaf of bread the servants have brought. Moving the blade away from the food, she dangles it over her wrist.

"It would be such an easy thing."

But she does not do it.

"It would be such a holy thing."

But she cannot do it.

"I'm damned," she says as she throws the knife down and flees the room. I wonder if she realizes how easily she is moving. If she knows that the lifeforce that feeds me is also feeding her. Since moving into Boaz's house, she looks ten years younger. Our neighbors say it is due to the easier life. I know otherwise.

She knows before I do that I am with child. She finds me throwing up and smoothes back my hair as if I was a child - *her* child.

"It will pass," she says.

"It better." But it does not. The child that I carry, that is my legacy to a world that would hate me if it understood me, drains my energy to such an extent I have to pull more life from Boaz. He begins to falter, his vitality fading as my belly grows.

Boaz barely survives to see his son born. He takes him from the midwife, his smile triumphant, and then I grab the child away as Boaz falls to the floor. The midwife rushes to him, and I try to look sad as she tells me that my husband is dead.

My son stirs, seeking my breast, and I smile at the brush of his spirit waiting to be freed. But then I feel him being pulled from my arms.

"What?"

Naomi has her robes open, her once old breasts now glisten with milk.

"Drink, child. Drink from me."

I scream as I feel the spirit of my son rush away from me and into Naomi. I try to grab him from her but she carries him away, the sound of his suckling like the drag of a chair over a stone floor.

"Hush, Ruth, your mother will take care of you now," the midwife says. She leans down, her hand gentle on my face. "We all know how kind you've been to her. How much you love her."

There is something in her eyes, and I reach down and realize I am bleeding.

"Lie still," Naomi says, "or you will surely die."

"As will you." I do not care that the midwife is hearing this. I do not care about anything.

"As will he, your begetter of kings."

I lie still. For I cannot lose him. Not now.

Naomi hands my child to me, and as soon as his mouth fastens on my breast, I can feel the pain inside me cease, and I know I've stopped bleeding.

The midwife looks at us as if we are both mad.

"My daughter-in-law is not from here, all this talk of kings," Naomi says. "But then you know that. Everyone knows about Ruth, my devoted little outsider." Naomi leans down, kisses my son, and whispers, "Wherever you go, I will go."

The curse does not work for her, not the same way it works for me. But my son stops suckling long enough to meet her eyes with his own. His are older than they should be; they see more clearly than a newborn's ought to.

Then they fasten on me. And they are filled with something else. It looks a bit like hate.

"His name is Obed," I say. It means servant. He will serve Naomi, not me. It fills me with pain to call him that, but it is a true name, and while I am evil, I am not blind to the truth. I touch his forehead and he starts to cry.

Naomi takes him from me and kisses me on the cheek.

"You'll always have a home with us, dear."

She is clearly enjoying this. I have definitely rubbed off on her.

The pain starts up again. I pull at Naomi's lifeforce, feel energy draining out of her, but the child is filling her with what he's draining from me.

I hear her laugh with delight. The baby gurgles. My son.

Her son.

I reach out with everything in me; feel some part of him respond. Then nothing.

Naomi lets the midwife leave, has the servants remove Boaz for burial. I lie in blood-soaked linens and wish so hard for oblivion that I can hear the dry wings of death approaching. But then I feel my son in my arms again and Naomi leaves him with me.

She is still tied to me. And she does not want to die. It's not much.

But it's enough for now.

Babylon's Burning
by Daniel Kaysen

"There'll be girls, Daniel," said my brother. "Loads of stunning girls."

What he meant was: whores. I'd heard about what happened at these company parties. Call girls were scattered about, and they were free-to-access, as it were.

I shivered slightly.

"You don't like the idea of girls?"

"I don't like the idea of Bell, Chase & Herr!"

In fact, they made my flesh crawl. They were big in International Security, which meant they were paid a vast amount of money, often by our government, to do unspeakable things at home and abroad.

No one ever went to jail.

My brother was just a headhunter there and he was a recent hire. So he didn't have blood on his hands. But I had principles. I *really* didn't want to go to their party.

"You're a writer," he said. "You could call it research."

He always mixed me up with a novelist or something.

"I translate poetry," I said.

Or I used to, when I was at University. Since graduating, I'd been working in a call center. It was hell, but I saw no way out.

"Yeah, well, you don't have to mention the poetry translation. Look, come for the girls. I mean, when did you last get laid?"

I'd been going out with Sarah for three years. She was great, but she was saving herself for marriage.

Of course, there's lots of other exciting things a couple can do, if one of them is saving herself for marriage.

We somehow didn't really do those either.

"I get laid plenty!" I said.

"Please, just come. I could use you, bro."

Turning up alone would look terrible for my brother, but he wasn't dating and he didn't have many real friends outside work, so who could he bring to the party but me?

For a headhunter, he wasn't very popular.

I was surprised to find I suddenly felt sorry for him. He was an unpopular headhunter at a horrible firm. And he was my brother, after all. Besides, he'd loaned me some money after University, which I still hadn't paid back.

"Okay," I said. "Okay. I'll come and prostitute myself for you."

"Great!" he said. "Thanks. But don't be too huffy when you're there. In fact, don't be huffy at all."

"What, like asking whether your company still outsources its torture? Or has it been brought back in-house?"

"Funny," he said.

Which we both knew didn't actually answer my question.

***

Oh my God, the girls.

Seriously.

The *girls*.

And they all seemed to be fresh from the Sorbonne or Harvard or somewhere.

Like the girl who introduced herself as Evelyn and turned out to have a Masters in Medieval Literature from

Oxford; an exceedingly rare chance for me to brag to someone who would understood what I did.

"Actually," I told her, "I published a modern verse translation of some of Chrétien de Troyes."

I said it as nonchalantly as I could.

"I'm impressed," she said, touching my arm. I know that whores aren't that hard to impress, but still.

"You okay, bro?" said my brother, suddenly at my side.

"We were talking about my translation of Chrétien de Troyes," I said.

He blinked.

"And you wonder why you *never* get laid," he said.

"I *do* get laid," I said, hastily. "I get laid loads."

Evelyn smiled. I wondered if she sensed this wasn't true.

"I'm sure there are lots of lucky women," she said. "In fact, I was hoping you might be free to be with me, tonight."

I nearly choked on my olive.

"Am I so ugly?" she said

"No, you're just..." I tried to find the right word. But I couldn't. "You're pre-paid."

She laughed, loud enough that it turned a lot of heads.

"Actually, I'm Evelyn Chase. Vice President, Forecasting."

"Wait," I said. "Wait."

I caught her by the bar.

"How can you work *here*, for this company?" I said. "Don't you find all this monstrous? The 'security' business?"

"You know, you're very sweet to care about my soul, but it's long since lost. How's yours?"

"Mine? I think I checked mine at the door," I said.

I looked around the crowd. There was an air of happy, edgy expectation. Maybe it was because so many men knew they were going to get laid - spectacularly.

A waiter came by and offered me a glass of champagne 'for the show'.

"What show?" I asked.

"You'll see," said Evelyn.

"Should be good," a guy said. He was rough hewn with an on-guard look, ready for anything.

"He a bouncer?" I whispered to Evelyn.

"Exorcist," she said. "We like to have them around in case things get interesting. Father Morton, this is Daniel."

We shook hands.

He was carrying the chalice you drink communion from, when you go to church. It was filled with champagne. It had a cocktail umbrella.

"Isn't that sacrilege?" I said.

"Oh, I'm sure *his* God can take a joke," Evelyn said.

"So who's *your* God?" I asked her. As soon as the words were out of my mouth I knew that I didn't want to know.

"We worship Gods of gold and silver, bronze and iron, wood and stone," she said. "They're the go-to Gods, for people like us."

I couldn't think of a single thing to say.

"Oh don't look so shocked, we do good works as well. Or good works of a sort." She laughed again.

And then there was a murmur from the crowd, animal and deep.

"The show," Evelyn said, pointing. There, on a raised stage by a white wall, stood a calm-looking woman, maybe five years older than me. Next to her stood a man with a gun in one hand and a sword in the other.

The crowd hushed.

The man raised the gun, and put it to the woman's head.

A total pin-drop hush came over the room.

He fired.

She fell.

The wall behind her was red.

To be honest, I wasn't very impressed.

I mean, call that a magic trick? A little paint-bomb behind her head, detonated at the right moment, it wasn't like it was difficult.

"What's the twist?" I whispered to Evelyn. This was Bell, Chase & Herr. Surely their cabaret should be top notch, not something a special effects man could cobble together in five minutes.

"The next bit is the twist," Evelyn said.

The man raised the sword above his head and swung it down and…

That wasn't really any more convincing. Her hand appeared to have been severed. It wasn't *her* hand of course. It was a plastic hand. Her hand, I knew, was hidden in her sleeve. Again, a special effects guy could have done it in five minutes.

"I don't get it," I whispered to Evelyn.

"Watch."

I watched.

The severed hand rose into the air.

It extended its index finger, which I had to concede was a neat trick, and it dipped its fingertip into the fake blood on the wall. And then it started writing a message in blood, on the perfect white wall.

It wrote:

Mene?

Mene?

Tekel! Upharsin.

When it had done the last full-stop, the hand fell to the floor and was still.

"They must have cut the strings," I whispered to Evelyn. I peered up at the ceiling to see if I could see where the strings had originated.

I wondered what happened next. The woman was just lying there, motionless. Surely now was the time to get up and take her bow. It was hardly the greatest cabaret I'd ever seen. Or maybe it was cutting edge performance art, a deliberately amateur show that was meant to be a deconstruction of war or capitalism - or performance art.

Whatever it was, it had to be more than a woman pretending to be dead for longer than was necessary.

"Now what happens?" I asked Evelyn.

"Now everyone interprets the writing wrong," she said. "Father Morton?"

Father Morton gave the bible version.

"Two and a half thousand years ago, Belshazzar was the ruler of Babylon, a wicked and pagan kingdom. A severed hand appeared at Belshazzar's great banquet, and wrote *Mene Mene Tekel Upharsin* on the wall. Daniel, the prophet, interpreted it as meaning that Belshazzar's deeds had been *Mene*, meaning numbered, and *Tekel*, meaning weighed and found wanting, so his kingdom would be *Upharsin*, which was a pun on the words for "divided" and "Persia." Belshazzar was slain the next day, and his kingdom was split between the Medes and the Persians."

"So what does tonight's writing mean?"

The speaker was a handsome white-haired man. The crowd around us was suddenly exceedingly still.

"Hey Daddy," said Evelyn, putting her arm round his middle.

So this was the big shot Mr. Chase. Big, big shot.

"Well, maybe it's a warning," said Father Morton, "like the company's going to be torn apart, Sir."

He couldn't quite make eye-contact while he said it.

"What about you, Tony? You agree?"

Evelyn whispered: "Soothsayer," as a non-descript man stepped forward from the crowd.

"On balance, yes, I agree, Sir. There's not much room for ambiguity."

"Well it's sounding great so far," said Chase senior, with a smile that was just a touch too wide. "Anyone got a different view?"

I coughed; he didn't hear.

But Evelyn did.

"Daniel has a different view, Daddy."

"Go on, son," said Chase, "what you got?"

"The words are biblical but the punctuation isn't," I said. "I think the use of question marks in *Mene? Mene?* and the exclamation mark in *Tekel!* changes the sense completely. I think it's like saying: 'Is it cold? No, it's *freezing!*' I think *Mene? Mene? Tekel!* is talking about something that will be so numerous that you won't be able to *count* it, you will have to *weigh* it instead."

"Like what?" he said.

"Like money, Sir. I think your company is going to enter into a venture that will make you so much money you will have to weigh it instead of counting it."

"What kind of venture, Son?"

"Well, the last word *Upharsin* meant Persia, Sir, and that was the old name for Iran. So I think there's going to be an invasion of Iran, Sir, and it's going to be awesome for your company."

He laughed.

"I do like a man who tells me what I want to hear. You're hired, as of now. You'll have your own staff."

"But..."

He held up his hand.

"Son, we worship Gods of gold and silver, bronze and iron, stone and wood. They give us guidance when we ask for it, but it's often unclear. We need people like you to help us to read the signs. There aren't many people like you. You've just been made Head of Prophecy."

Something caught my eye across the room. It was my brother, raising his glass to me.

"But..."

"Evey will answer your questions," said Mr Chase.

"But..."

And he was gone.

***

It was me and Evelyn, surrounded by the sounds of a happy party: chatter, music, ice in glasses.

The woman on the stage still lay motionless, in a pool of fake blood.

"Now, *she's* got a shitty job," I said, to Evelyn.

"You're smiling," she said.

"I *am* smiling," I said. "I don't think I ever found anything so satisfying to translate. It's like, that was a *real* challenge. It's amazing. Who thought up that test? Is there like some guy you employ just to set translation exams?"

She looked at me.

"I passed the test!" I said. "I aced it. No one else did. Damn I feel good."

"Good enough to go upstairs with me?"

Well obviously I wasn't going to go upstairs with her. Obviously I wasn't going to do that. Or if I was, it wasn't going to get physical. It wasn't going to be sex. Not even a kiss.

I mean, obviously.

***

I screamed her name three times before the dawn.

***

Gods of gold and silver, bronze and iron, stone and wood looked down on me.

***

I was far beyond any further feeling: so many pleasure receptors had burnt out; so many pain ones too.

After that shock and awe, at last I saw the truth.

The severed hand wasn't special effects, I knew that now. The words were not written by a guy who set translation tests.

"Who was the woman?" I said as the sun broke the horizon. "The one who was killed in the show."

Evelyn ran her fingers through my hair.

"She used to work here. And she was a virgin," she said. "The death of innocence fuels the messages. Did you know that?"

Innocence.

Innocents.

The Gods of gold and silver, bronze and iron, stone and wood looked down on me.

I thought back over what had just happened.

Evelyn and I had done all the things that couples do when one of them is saving himself for marriage. And a dozen other things that don't make the books you find in stores.

She and I had done everything, except the main event.

"Why didn't we have sex?" I said.

"Because you're still a virgin."

"Ha," I said. "No way."

On this one I was on solid ground.

"Me and Callie Westerbrook. June 15th, four years ago. She was a waitress at the beach-side restaurant, I was a kitchen porter. We did it on the dunes in the moonlight one night."

"You didn't have intercourse," she said.

"I did! Find her and ask her."

"We did find her and ask her," she said. "Callie told us that the sex you had was intercrural. You were thrusting into her pushed-together thighs. She didn't want to get pregnant, and she guessed you wouldn't know the difference."

She looked at me.

The Gods looked at me.

The room was very, very quiet.

"I'm still a *virgin*?"

She nodded.

I thought about all the research that had gone into establishing that I had never actually had sex.

My brother had been in on it, of course. And then he maneuvered me here. Perhaps he wasn't such a sorry headhunter after all.

Because they'd got their prophet. I'd walked right into their trap.

Almost.

"I haven't accepted the job, yet," I said.

"Oh, but you will. You're going to have so much fun. The translation work is fascinating. And the girls, I tell you. You're going to love them."

"But they won't ever have full sex with me?"

"No. That would kill your power of prophecy."

"So what's stopping me just going to a club and picking someone up?"

"Well, the guards here, for one thing. This building is your home now."

Something very cold passed over me.

"Can I leave at all?"

"No. We like to keep our prophecy in-house."

She said it calmly.

"So what happens if I try to leave right now, this minute?"

She laughed. "You wouldn't make it to the lift."

I believed her. I tried not to panic.

"Look," I said, "Believe me. Whatever you want, you can have it. Let me just go back to my old life, okay? This is a mistake. You've got the wrong man. I'm not corporate. I'm not a drone. I'll go nuts, I won't be any use. Let me just go back to Sarah. We'll move abroad…"

"Sarah's dead, I'm afraid."

"*Dead*? Of what?"

"Of several bullets, and some other stuff."

I squinted at her in disbelief.

"Daniel, your DNA and prints are everywhere at the crime scene, in all the most incriminating places. Like on the knife, and the ropes. It was horrible what you did. If you're caught and tried, you'll be the darling of the prison block. You'll be raped in your cell, day and night. Sarah was a virgin angel and you murdered her. You did some other bad things to her body, too. Seriously, you don't ever want to leave here."

The trouble was I believed her. I had no doubt that Bell, Chase & Herr would happily murder anyone to get their way, or to make their point - or just have some fun.

"The upside," said Evelyn, "is that we got another message on the wall, from her blood. But we can't translate it. You want to hear the message?"

I knew that if I said yes then I would be accepting the job.

The Gods of gold and silver, bronze and iron, stone and wood, looked down on me.

Their mouths were frozen, but I knew they had so much to say. So much. So much.

And only I could help them get it out.

It would take death, of course. The endless death of innocence.

It would be carnage, always.

But the power I would have. The things I would see.

"What's it like?" I whispered to her.

"It's like this," she said.

Her fingers closed my eyes, and the gods showed me their plans.

I saw a small boy walking down the street, as a bomb went off next to him, blowing him apart.

I heard a journalist talking, sincerely, of Freedom and Peace.

I smelled napalm and meat and sweat in the twilight.

I touched the flesh of the wanton dead, and the willing living.

I tasted the ashes of skyscrapers that I had helped bring down.

Then the vision ended.

I opened my eyes.

I longed to go again.

"So?" she said.

All that power.

All that burning power would be mine, if I accepted. But I knew, too, that it would hollow me out.

He who channels those Gods will pay.

A mind can only see so much, before it catches fire.

"What happens when I can't do it anymore?" I said.

"You die with dignity, calmly, on the stage, and your successor will interpret what's written in your blood."

So. The woman was the previous Head of Prophecy.

Babylon had never been destroyed. It had simply changed with the times, guided by the Gods that had never gone away.

"If I say yes, what happens *after* I die?"

Heaven seemed irrelevant. Hell too parochial.

"You would go to the land of the Gods."

"And what's that like?"

"Cruel, and wonderful."

"I can't imagine that," I said.

But I could. I really could.

"So? Daniel?" she said.

So.

I knew I should say no.

I knew I should seek terrible vengeance on the company for what they did to Sarah. I knew I should go out all guns blazing, in revolt at the overwhelming evil they so casually employed. But everyone can be bought. Everyone has a price.

And they knew mine. It wasn't even money.

I closed my eyes in defeat and acceptance.

I took the job, as we both knew I would.

I said: "Tell me what they wrote in Sarah's blood."

***

After I had translated it, Evelyn did something new to my body as the sun rose higher, and the diligent workers of Bell, Chase & Herr started their new day, and more of my pain and pleasure receptors began to wither and fail, and the Gods of gold and silver, bronze and iron, stone and wood, looked down on their new hire, and faraway the war machines began to board their ships, and women, who would soon be widowed and childless, woke from happy dreams.

As if Favorites of their God
By Christi Krug

I remember her eyes that cold spring morning, eyes of grey that quivered and changed; the way she looked at me, straight and still. It was the day I would learn of my end. That day I would eat my fear, swallow it whole, line my gut with it. My eternity would be set.

For Temborah, the morning was like any other. She and her apprentice, Hermuth, did their work in that hovel of an excuse for a house. Temborah showed Hermuth the herbs they would sort and mix. They began their work, hands flying. Hermuth pierced her finger on a thorn, and heard herself swearing by the gods. Temborah glanced up, quick.

"I don't believe in the gods," said Temborah.

"But you're a witch." Hermuth looked at the tall woman in the grey shift. "You *must* believe in the gods."

Temborah closed her eyes, tilted back her head and rolled her loose black curls salted with white. "I don't have to believe in anything. Yes, I see the spirits. I speak with the dead. I can look beyond this shallow, thin world of ours. But I don't believe in any deities, especially the petty Hebrew god."

Hermuth shook out her fingers, picked up her pestle. She pulverized the yellow buds. A bouquet filled the air: the gentle sweetness of chamomile and the brightness of anise, the spice of cinnamon and the decay of bone and bark. Temborah nodded at the progress of her helper.

When she then sorted clumps of herbs, she stopped for a moment.

"Perhaps I would not spurn the Hebrew god," Temborah offered, "if I understood the god's followers. But the spirits of the Hebrew holy ones don't behave as they should. When they die, instead of hovering near the earth, they disappear, like mists before the sun on Lake Kinneret. As if they are favorites of their god, who cannot bear to be without them. They can never be reached after they die." She reached up to a high ledge and took down several clay jars. She inspected them, arranged them on the table. "As if they are too good for the grave, too good for this world."

Hermuth nodded and passed her bowl, then took up the next bundle of dried herbs, untying the twine and breaking the flowered heads into an urn.

Temborah raised her brows in a show of carelessness.

"Since I cannot speak with such spirits," she said, "I have no way to judge the god of the Hebrews. Whether their god is just, or merciful. Or whether this god exists at all." She poured the freshly ground powder into the mouth of the jar, tapping a finger to sift it down the long neck. "Surely this god does not care for the living." She nodded inward to the hut. "The stories of these Hebrews, their king, and the commands their god gives - they are terrible. The laws. I'll never understand."

She shook her head and laughed a single bitter laugh.

Hermuth began to reply, then steadied her bottom lip with her teeth. She knew how the king's laws had caused the death of Temborah's own grandmother at the hands of Hebrew soldiers, forty years ago.

Temborah held her head high, looking down through her long eyelashes. Hermuth marveled how, despite Temborah's scars, she was vibrant and lovely.

"I can bring strength to the withered thigh," said Temborah, "can brighten the eye once dimmed, and cleanse the leper with my tonics." She wrapped one hand around the jar. "I know the path of blood in a man. I can embitter or sweeten water, and can knead a woman's foot to open her womb." She held the jar aloft, a faint smile on her lips.

"But I don't understand this god of the Hebrews," Temborah finished, "and clearly *she* does not understand me."

Hermuth held her pestle in midair. She stared at Temborah, her shawl slipping from her shiny rolling shoulders. Temborah reached over and took the pestle and bowl from her younger helper. Finally Hermuth managed a whisper, "They'll kill you for such words. You cannot call their god a woman."

"Chaff!" said Temborah. "I will say what I will say. The Hebrews would kill me if they knew of my arts. I am no longer a child to be wrenched away from everything she knows, and married off to a fool."

She tipped another bowl of powder into a tall jar.

"My life is forfeit if they find me. At least now I practice my arts. For a little while."

She stared at the swirled powders, wondering silently what had changed. These last few years, she rarely heard the spirits. Hers was a great sadness, a heart like an empty bowl.

Later Temborah put Hermuth to sweeping the dirt floor, and set a pot to boil. A strange creature hobbled through the open door. A reject of animals. A crazed duck with bird feet, legs long and bright red as if dipped in blood. Flapping one wing, the animal cried in a wheezy caw.

Temborah smiled at the creature then yelled back at

Hermuth. "Throw some grain in the yard for Zipporah, will you? I'm off to the market for fish hearts."

***

For me, the morning began in the middle of the night. With a headache, and much work to do. The leather ties would not fasten in my fingers. "Dammit, get me a cloak that fits!" I yelled, and threw the garment to my floor where it made a silken puddle on the polished acacia. I went through my trunk again.

"Ridiculous!" I muttered. Such pains I took to get attention anymore.

My steward, Fashev, pursed his lips, looking down.

"I'm sorry, my King."

"And now," I said, "I must go tramping through the wilderness to find *someone* who can talk to God, any god for that matter. Anyone willing to offer one little word. After all the nights I've gone without sleep, food, drink, all the wounds of my body and soul, all for my subjects, my Kingdom!"

"Yes, King," said Flashev, holding out a cloak. I opened my arms and allowed him to draw up the sleeves, and a sigh tore through me.

"Nothing," I said. "Not a single word of prophecy, a song or a dream. I can't even find a witch when I need one."

"But sire," said Fasheve, "you banished all witches, under penalty of death. Witchcraft is a sin according to Moses."

"I know the Law! And I know what I said. I would've expected someone to have the foresight to spare just one in case of need."

I shook my head.

42

"Just trying to do the right thing. Just *trying* to stay in the favor of the One. I didn't ask to be here, I remind Him. I didn't ask to be made King. It was all his idea - and Samuel's." That was all I could say for several moments. The name turned in my stomach. I scanned the ceiling, the walls, suddenly afraid. As if by saying the name of the prophet, I had uttered an abomination.

I looked at the clothes spilling from the open trunk. "There," I said, pointing to a bundle of cloth on the floor. "That turban. I'll take it."

"Very well, Lord."

***

The night air was cold but there was a warmth in the breeze - a warmth that circled the body without penetrating the skin; sickened rather than cheered for it carried the smell of carrion and decay.

I trudged forward into the darkness. What a place: Endor. Time was I never would have set foot in a crust of a place like Endor. But there I was. King of a holy nation. With a God who had abandoned his people, for surely if God didn't speak to the King, what of the people? They were all lost.

Most on my mind was the young man who made me feel like weeping, raging, taking my own life or his. There was a purity about him, a beauty. He was everything I could have been. And the world loved him. God loved him. He was using them all, using *God* even, to distract, to taunt me. I rubbed my temples. Hair was wet on my forehead, slipping from my turban. *Saul has killed his thousands, but David his ten thousands.* The song, the sickening song drove the headache.

God's anointed should carry out the work of God without this madness.

I felt the mud pulling at the soft doeskin straps of my sandals. The sandals I had made. The gazelle I myself had slain. So fleet I was, to catch the animal. And I was virile. My wives moaned in my arms.

Ah, that gazelle - how awkwardly it had loped, blood spilling from its mouth, the supple hide rolling forward, the stuck arrow swinging with its gait. The beast was pregnant. Cook made a fine stew of those supple, unborn creatures.

I could almost taste the salt, in the dark of this God-forsaken journey. It was such a long way. I trudged onward; my men keeping their distance - Hezob ahead - and Fashev behind. A long way to go to find a witch.

At my feet was a black pall, a thin sheen of deep red that flowed over and through the muddy ruts. I looked to the sky. The moon had a red cast. An odd night. Surely I could inquire about it to the Chief Astrologer, had I not killed the Chief Astrologer.

Or rather, the other Saul had killed him. That other, younger me. An untested king bent on following every law, so sure of himself as the hand of God, to bless His chosen people. I remembered, as a young king kneeling on the frozen ground to chip and smash and hack the wooden face of an idol, hating it with every blow. It was the day I had cleansed my house. I found the idol in a servant's things. I was then a man who could kneel in the gravel, though his knees bled, certain that the eyes of God rested upon his shoulders.

My face itched. My nerves were shot. It was the effect of the Philistine midnight raids, the knifings, the screams of men who had never in their lives screamed. My stomach clenched. I felt the fluids and biles. Oh, to have the strong, clean body of my youth. Back in those days when I did everything a king should.

The warm draft broke apart in the cold night air; sounds echoed in the distance. A scream. Some bird, with a voice that keened in agony, it should have been put to death, should have been wrung until its eyes popped.

I longed for the memories; the face of David, and my own boy, singing the stupid chants of women. I wished for music. Anything that might soothe.

"Hezob!" I called out. "What did you bring to drink?"

"Only water, my Lord."

"Why?"

"You decreed so, my Lord. In voyages by night only water should be carried, lest stupor overtake the soldiers who'd die of cold."

"Never mind the decree! Is there no one who can think of a King's needs?"

As we went on, a tiny demon of a muscle tugged at my left eye. A twitch I had of late. I slapped it. The weariness. God has left me, so the people said. I could slap at flies that were not there.

The ground sloped as we marched, skirting Mount Tabor. We climbed. There was the dead bracken of winter; the wisps of clouds forming dirty shreds in the blackness. All was still. I had my flask at my side, but little was left to sip.

I couldn't deny the feeling of being pursued like a dog. The stench again. Like the stench of death that surrounded Nob, which at the time was satisfying, so satisfying; which at the time told me I had done everything I could do, had severed every head of the traitorous priests who had harbored David. Priests in their wickedness, betraying their King, the hand of God in the world.

This stench was sour and sweet. Sickly. I pulled my dark plain cloak around me. The ground began to slope and we descended in the icy air; crackling layers covered the mud like unleavened bread.

A young woman opened the door to our party. She was Hermuth. Her eyes opened wide. It had been a long time since they'd seen visitors from the village. And they knew we were not villagers.

Hezob spoke.

"My master seeks your services."

Hermuth held the door. Temborah stepped forward, having just returned from market. She examined us carefully. No, we weren't from around there. Temborah bowed her head, buying a moment.

"I - I do not practice anymore," she said. "Only when I was a child, apprenticed to my ill-fated grandmother. I could not help that."

All this wait and decorum and deception, just for a word from spirits. I stepped forward.

"Never mind that," I said. "You *will* help me. We need a medium."

Temborah looked up, grey eyes like frozen pools. The color drained from her face. "Are you trying to destroy me?"

I shook my head.

"I promise you. No one will know of this."

My mouth was dry.

Temborah shifted her weight, smoothed her dress. I would learn about it later: how, just then, she began to feel the presence of horror. Her feet were cold as stone. She felt thin and brittle, but nodded quietly.

"All right."

She led us inside, offering her worn, red cushions. My men took their posts in the corners. I sat. I tried to assure her with a gentle smile.

"What is it you want?" she said.

"I am here to contact the Judge and Prophet, Samuel. I seek wisdom from him."

Samuel? Temborah pursed her lips to taste the name. She turned fluidly, lit a punk from the fire; then lit the lamp, set it on a table. She'd done all this scores of times, she reminded herself. She would motion with her hands, speak the words of incanting, ask a question. There would be nudges. A heat or a chill, and a sigh or a smack of a tree branch. She would nod and interpret. But in the last few years the spirits did not visit, and neither did the villagers. The spirits turned their faces from her, leaving nothing to interpret. Not even the tick of an insect wing, or the glowing of an ember.

She looked down and saw that her hands were trembling.

Indeed, her hands both dark and graceful were shaping mysterious figures. Her witch's teeth, white as milk, appeared through a gaping hole in her lips, a remnant of her scarring. She had been treated poorly as a young bride.

I could not know it but my presence had reminded her of that time.

Temborah could see her fat husband, red-faced, chasing her through the yard. "What do you think you're doing?" He gritted his teeth, seized her elbow, yanked her into the house, where he kicked at the fire she had made that morning, emptied her jars of unguents. He threw them at the walls and into her face. Her skin blazed hot and red. The humiliation. The pain. She stood against the wall of the house, immobile, screaming, her hair blazing, dripping like wax.

After that night, the Hebrews took her husband into their army, where the Philistines speared him.

Temborah looked down at the packed red dirt of her home and closed her eyes, pulling and kneading with her hands, the shapes that once would bring spirits. In this case, she thought to invent a voice for this Samuel. It would not be difficult. There was never an answer from the God.

I waited, dumb and still, my mind racing. And then came a horrible keening. I felt all my muscles seize up, like a man trying to run in a dream. My God, what was it?

"Hermuth!" Temborah called to the back of the house, behind the curtain. "Remove Zipporah to the shed. And you may go away for the day."

The assistant scrambled outside.

As soon as it began, the noise stopped.

Temborah closed her eyes again. Her breathing stilled. Together we waited in the darkness with curtains drawn.

Years later, Temborah would tell me how something felt very wrong. Something was alive. Her stomach tightened. She felt herself disconnect from the world.

There was a cinder in the left wall; a cinder in the very place where her husband had flung sulfur and quicksilver into her face. A cinder where her husband had shoved her head against the mud bricks until her mouth had run with blood. A cinder, like a tiny worm, opening, glowing. Growing.

A sickness whirled in her stomach and she tried not to cry out. When she opened her eyes, the face of Ehluch stared at her - the round, glib chin in the curling beard, the small ears and piggy eyes.

"No!" She put her face in her hands, trying to catch her breath.

I watched her, stunned by the emotion.

"You see him?"

My voice cracked. I felt cold and dirty, and full of hope.

"Does he speak?"

I could no longer contain myself. I fell to the ground.

"My lord," I said, to the place where Temborah was looking. "My lord! May the Almighty bless you!"

I spoke to silence, the quivering air.

And then a low, strangled voice, like a calf with a rope around its neck, or a maimed, deformed thing gurgling. The thing did not belong.

"Why?" it said.

My body went cold. I was blind to the sight. Samuel. To see and be seen. To witness the slow, slight smile, to hear the offer of atonement, a new chance, a new day. I would no longer be alone.

Temborah squinted and held herself back. Eluch was swallowed up in a bright flame, enveloped by a skin that peeled open to nothing. Now the presence before her was garbed in the robe of a holy man. She placed both hands upturned on her knees, bowed her head, saw her own palms reflected red in the light, their lines branched and broken. There was more at stake than her life. Always she had avoided the fate of the people in her adopted lands. Prophets did not come for such as she. They came for Kings.

I heard Temborah gasp as she sat upright. She turned to me. "You...you are Saul!"

There was fear in her eyes, but hate as well. After all, I was the one responsible for the killing of her grandmother.

A trap, she thought. But then, she must have seen the whiteness in my face. The wildness of my eyes.

"Please!" I begged. "Let me hear the Prophet!"

The spirit stooped like an old man, and its robes trailed along the ground but did not quite touch it, like a skein of oil on the surface of the lake.

"I have done all that God has asked," I offered to this presence. In my ears my voice sounded too young, like a whining boy. "But the prophets will not speak. God withholds his signs. The Philistines grow strong against me."

Temborah drew her heels beneath her, sat back. This was not her husband. No. This was something the like of which she had never seen.

Again, the strangled wheeze. Like a snuffling animal beyond the grave.

"It does not avail you, Saul," said the apparition. Only Temborah could see him and what she saw was a tall, diseased willow. The skin was white, peeling bark; long hairs fell thinly over head and brows. The thing had a knob for a nose, the stripped look of a calf's skeleton. It smelled acrid like the poison white mushroom.

Temborah felt hot fluid rising in her throat.

"You have rebelled," said Samuel. "To rebel is as the sin of witchcraft!"

I could not speak.

A few feet from me, Temborah's flesh prickled. She was afraid and perplexed. Why was she not destroyed?

"But I slayed the Almelekites!" I managed. My voice grew louder, once I had mustered it. "I banished the witches!" I pounded the floor with my fist. It was all I could think of. How right I had been. How just. I looked toward the wall searching, because I could not see what the Witch of Endor saw.

And this, this was not any conjuring she had ever done. Yet it was so, a reminder of how she used to hear the miraculous whisperings of the deceased.

Samuel the Prophet sneered at me.

"You will die at the hand of the Philistines. You and your sins."

Then he turned his back, and like a stick insect, slowly, limb by limb stepped down into a blackness, a liquid blackness roiling and spinning. Almost, Temborah could see him disintegrate into yellowed, withered bones, could follow a dark, thick ooze that boiled from the earth, pitted by flesh bits from the the myriad dead. A hand. A head spliced in half. A child's head wedged in the mouth of a long-haired skeleton.

Temborah covered her eyes.

The candle went out.

I collapsed onto the floor, mouth open, but could make no sound. Temborah sat, holding the stub of the lantern's candle.

"It appears your god hates both of us," she said. She knelt and touched my hand.

"King."

If I had been aware, perhaps I would have caught the tone of mockery. My servants were in the corner, blinking, staring wide-eyed. They looked at each other perhaps taking comfort in their mutual sickness.

"Sire?" whispered Flashev.

I did not move.

"King," said Temborah. This time her voice was soft, but I did not answer. I have no recollection of those long hours in which my eyes did not see, my ears did not hear and my mind filled with the horror of the forsaken.

"King!" Temborah and the servants kept calling to me.

Finally, as if from far away, a soft, high sound opened my own throat.

Temborah shook her head. This she understood.

"You are undernourished, my lord. You are weak and need food."

She took me by the arm and sat me upon the reed mats beside her table. Even then, how she needed my company!

"Eat."

"Eat, eat!" said the men in unison.

She brought before me bread and veal. Roasted meat, so fresh. I ate like one in a dream. There was nothing to say. Afterward I stood, loosening the belt around my cloak. I nodded to my men. They followed me through the door into an afternoon of shadows.

I turned once, placed five silver coins on her door stone. Then we turned and strode away.

Alone in her house, Temborah sat numb. She broke off a chunk of the bread she had baked and chewed slowly.

I was dead within the week.

And then I returned to that hut, to my new and only friend, the one who would always listen.

Psalm of the Second Body
By Catherynne Valente

Go, and bring the harlot, Shamhat, with you.
When the animals are drinking at the watering place
have her take off her robe and expose her sex.
When he sees her he will draw near to her,
and his animals, who grew with him in wildness,
will be alien to him.

- The Epic of Gilgamesh
First Tablet

I am the first story ever told: the story of the harlot.

This story was always mine - pine boughs prickling at my breasts, cedar-smells exuding from my pores like a temple censer, the smooth curve of my forearms extended in the shadow-wood. I am not the prolegomena, I am the poem. I am the story before Gilgamesh, the verses scratched from the clay tablet to make room for him, and for the giant, the pastoral boar-ape, the coarse-bearded golem he loved.

But I had him first.

How he wished he could have done it! Laid out his body under Enkidu and sheared the hair from his body with a kiss! But he could not, he could only bluster and pray for it to happen, for a man to come with biceps as big as his. He called to me, in the depths of my temple, white in column and stair, he called me out of the city, beyond the sliver bolts and cedar slats of the Enlil Gate, he called me into the wild and the wold. Among my sisters who had grown with me in wildness, I prepared myself. I clothed myself in red veils;

53

my nipples shone through the fabric like eyes, my sex
throbbed in the crisp folds like a heart.

> (The harlot has a second body,
> which is like the first, but not the first.
>
> The organs are bewildered:
>
> the tongue is an ear which hears only gasps,
> the small of the back is a tongue
> which tastes the earth,
> the belly is a mouth which gulps and chews.
>
> She wears both bodies,
> like the sleeves of a dress,
> and pulls at the stitches when she must.)

I went out from the city of Uruk, whose streets cloud
with the dust of black-flanked horses and ash-wheeled carts.
I went out from the city of Uruk, whose walls were like the
moon - they waxed and waned with the whim of
Gilgamesh. I went out from the city of Uruk, which
languished in the summer heat, panting like a fat dog. I
went out from the lion-torches of the Ishtar Gate, into the
wild and the wold.

I could not perform my womb-dialogue in the sling
of the city, with tenements as my witnesses and the snorting
of oxen to time the rhythm of my hips. I sought out the
steppe, the wood, the bed of branches. I needed no guide, no
man to force open my legs - that is a lie of Gilgamesh, who
could not bear that I went out to Enkidu in eagerness, and
Enkidu came into me with eagerness, and there was no
thought of the King in that place.

Psalm of the Second Body by Catherynne Valente

I sought out the smell of the clay-spattered Nephil, the unfinished man - I knew instinctively how he would smell, how the musk of his hair would remember itself to my white nose, how the sour tang of his sweat would not be unlike the incense of my clean-stepped temple, how he would crawl among the greenery like a salamander seeking the cool of a muddy creek-bed.

The flowers of our arboreal stage were deep and red, so red as to be black, and the surface of the rippled lake was blue as paint. Primal colors: green and dirt and the grass-blades waving, the white-misted sky bruised by tips of cypress and pine whose bark smelled of skin. Into all this I walked with my scarlet veils streaming, into all this I walked with my hair trailing black against my calves, into all this I walked with silver rings on my toes, brown as dust but not as earth. Would the animals be afraid, touched by harlot-fingers, the perfumed forearms of the finished woman, her tongue all tattooed with arcana and codes of conduct?

They looked up, fawn and tortoise, crow and fox, lazy alligator sunning its cretaceous stomach, hare with ears like cubits, infant lion, grouse and quail and quill-tailed pheasant. They looked up, a constellation of liquid eyes, and looked away again, without concern. The fox lapped at the pool, the crocodile eyed the fox in hunger, the crow hopped from one grey foot to the other. Why should beasts who rut in seed-blown rye run from the red-veiled mare in heat?

The giant, boulder-backed and moss-shouldered, shadowed himself in the wood, thirsty, but wary of the new thing haunting the water. Enkidu sniffed the air for me, his beard tangled with sap and berries. He tried to taste the smell with the tip of his untried tongue. He peered from the patterned pine-shade and his eyes drank my red.

She Nailed a Stake Through His Head

(The harlot holds her second body
before her first.

It is the second body,
with its confused limbs,
that makes men love her,
makes their singular,
undoubled bodies
turn towards her like compass-needles.

They could not love her
if she held her eyes in her face,
only when she secrets them
away in her nipples,
blinking from atavistic lids.

They could not love her
if she arranged her flesh like theirs.

The original body is too terrifying -
the artificial self is reassuring.

The harlot is, after all, not like them.
She is feline, cephalopod, arachnid.
She is all wrong, inhuman.

Thus can men loathe her enough
to love her safely.)

I pulled veils from my limbs like husks, like blood
washed clean.

Psalm of the Second Body by Catherynne Valente

I know I am beautiful - the harlot must be absolutely honest about such things. When I am naked, my skin shines very softly with the nacreous light of Ishtar, my calves curve like the slats of a lyre, my lips part slightly and exhale the night-breath of welcome. When I was a girl, the temple-women would sigh over my hair, its black-bright length. Now it is the chief organ of my second body, its curls have their own mouths, whisper their own litanies. Enkidu's muscled hands twitched to pull it like the rope of a bell, to silence the mouths and feel them rustle over his savage thighs.

He came out of the cedar thatch hesitantly, like a sparrow hopping. The bristle-furred lion nuzzled up under his hand, snuffling for spare bits of food, but he ignored it, reaching his colossal arms out to me, ridiculously like a baby groping for its mother. His mouth hung open helplessly, but of course he had no language, no speech to beg me to fasten my legs around him. He was not even sure what it was he wanted - he was an infant, a son suckling at my breast. And indeed, he loped across the whistling grass and dropped to his scabbed knees, pushing his lips at me with the instinctive greed of a newborn turning its head towards the warm flow of milk. I tousled his hair; my hand came away sticky with loam and brackish sweat.

> (The harlot's second body is an amphora —
> it exudes all liquid.
> Blood, sweat, spit, come, milk —
> all of these are layered in her
> like sedimentary rock.
>
> This is part of her mystery.

She Nailed a Stake Through His Head

Her body is a flooded world,
a world without sleep,
a sea of fluid without land.
She is a city in the midst of this sea,
and her miraculous flesh
divides the waters.)

The first time he came right away. I pulled him over me and the red-tailed birds scattered up to the sky. His eyes closed and opened, closed and opened, and on his forehead I wrote the names of his parents, his first selves. His teeth quivered in his prognathous jaw, feeling suddenly the echo of his mother in him - and who could have been the mother of this rough-molded beast? What giantess crouched in the hills and tore his umbilicus with her teeth? Gilgamesh proclaimed that he was shaped from clay, that he alone of men was never clutched by the shadows of the womb - but the harlot knows better. No one escapes that blackness.

The record of his blood I scribed over his skull: *Aruru, Anu, Ninurta.*

This was the First Tablet.

The second time, I lay over him and the hare leapt up from the singing water. His nostrils flared and he pressed his face into my hair. My oiled mouths stamped out the code of law on his cheek: *Thou shalt not, thou shalt not, thou shalt not. Shall* is the law of the harlot, the law of the second body - *shalt not* is the law of Gilgamesh-who-let-the-walls-fall. My tongue traced out the ideographs of Hammurabi, of Solon, of Moses - and he groaned with the weight of the golden letters, left on his skin like the tracks of a jeweled snail. For the first time he felt as though he should not touch me, that the second body was wicked and dank -

and he grinned with the pleasure as he broke the clay law slabs by the bucking of my hips.

This was the Second Tablet.

The third time, he drew the milk from my breast and clamped his teeth upon me. The lion sniffed the air with a dripping muzzle and drew away from the water's edge. My tongue gave his tongue breath - a door opened in my womb and from it came the strands of cuneiform, delicate as insects, triangular heads bobbing with grace. I gave him hieroglyphs and pictograms and vowels with toes of glass. Phonemes, consonants like scarabs, and halting glottals poured from me to him, salt passed from vessel to vessel. I gave him 22 symbols, then 24, then 26. He became pregnant with my seed, fat with words, verses, stanza-zygotes fluttering next to his heart. On his chest the thin-stroked alphabet burned, and he spoke into the ear of my tongue, his voice thick and creaking as a new wheel, and the first word of the Edenic monster was my name:

Shamhat. Shamhat. Shamhat.

This was the Third Tablet.

The fourth time, he lay his head on my belly and his babbling drove the grouse and the fox underground. His beard shriveled into his face, dying like grass. His hair grew sleek and scented with cinnamon, his gnarled body smoothed itself into beauty. On his flesh sprouted leather and cotton, deerskin and silver bracelets like vines twisting up from quenched soil. His eyes lost their pupil-less gleam, their feral boil, and became soft as a hide, smudged with ink, lashes curled. His feet sandaled themselves and his calves greaved in bronze. He was become beautiful, like me, and the mark of me was on him like a weal, and he was not angry to lose innocence, but threw it off with a horse-like laugh, proud to be like I was.

Shamhat, take me with you into Uruk-Haven, and never leave me.

This was the Fourth Tablet.

The fifth time, the alligator slipped under the surface of the pool. I took him in my mouth and chanted the liturgy of numbers, so that he could count out seven jars of black beer, eleven copper coins, four cubits and five, two measures of honey and two of oil, seventeen slaves with golden eyes, nine silver fish on a line, three chairs at a single table, eleven tablets of clay, two gates to the city, six days and seven nights in the grip of my body, one Shamhat, one Enkidu. I taught him what *zero* was, the great secret Gilgamesh and all his sons could not touch, and showed him how his navel made this sign. I showed him how my mouth made this sign, and my womb made it, and his irises made it, and how his skull made it, and all his bones.

This was the Fifth Tablet.

The sixth time, I stretched out my body over his head and made of my skin a roof, and he dwelled within the house of me, safe from the prickling rain. He hid from the sky which wore its stars like a spray of blood. He hid from the trees and the eyes of the animals. He closed the doors of my thighs behind him and lay within a hut spattered with his voice, which he tried on everything like a teething child: *Wall. Woman. Fire. Mine. Enkidu.* And Shamhat, always Shamhat, his aleph, his first and favorite word. He closed himself away inside me and his scent changed. The animals did not hate him - what should they care that a beast mated with another beast? This was a lie of Gilgamesh, so that Enkidu would think I poisoned the wild against him, and love only his King in the warm and the dark. They thought it strange that he slept in a house, and no longer smelled of the moist soil and the rain puddling below the cypress boughs. He went into another herd, and smelled of the musk of its mare. But that was a thing the wild understood, and they nosed for their own mates under thickets and behind stones.

This was the Sixth Tablet.

The seventh time, I took his hands and placed them between my second body and my first, and the tortoise slept in its shell.

(The second body lies over the first.

It is not a shield, but a cloud.
It surrounds the first body,
conceals it so that the fingers
which stroke the misplaced limbs
of the second body
never penetrate to the first.

The space between them is filled with rain.
It is filled with fur and seeds.
It is filled with star-wattle.

The bodies are connected, they move
together, like twins within their mother.
Within them, only the cunt remains
in its right place.
It is the sun, and the bodies, planetary,
revolve around its light.

The space between them is the source
of the harlot's power. In the play
of the two bodies, the touch of heel to hair,
she creates herself over and over

She Nailed a Stake Through His Head

like the breathing of air
into a clay pot.)

In the space between the bodies, strewn with seed and stars, I traced words with his fist clamped in mine, shaping the letters with him, so that he learned to write for himself and to make words out of space, to initiate the first stroke of his own characters, which is the last of all things he learned:

I will go into Uruk for Uruk is the body of man, and when I have left the body of woman, Uruk will take me in and close me off from her, and I will know what it is to serve and to follow, I will know what it is to kill great things, and perform the change of Shamhat on the King of Uruk, who is Gilgamesh, who is son of Rimat-Ninsun, who will crack the horns of the Bull of Heaven, for no man shall have horns more splendid than his. I will go into Uruk for Uruk is the body of man, and I will wrap myself in its limbs, and I will forget the wild and the wold.

This was the Seventh Tablet.

For seven nights Enkidu did not sleep, but drank and drank until he was full of the draughts of Uruk, which passed through me and down his throat like sighs. He rolled in his satisfaction, the juices of language dribbling down his chest.

(Only the second body
can perform this metamorphosis.

The body of Ishtar
the harlot holds before her like a mirror—

Gilgamesh,
who has but one flesh,

62

envies it and loathes it
and dreams of crushing it
between his fingers.

He could not teach the golem-giant
to fashion words like stone hammers,
could not teach him to belong to Uruk.

He would never forget that he had to use me
to bring a brother behind the crumbling
walls.)

Enkidu followed me like a patient dog, though the beasts nosed his flanks and whimpered for him to stay and breed, now that his mare had come. Enkidu did not look at them. He followed me into the Uruk-Haven, into the market where jugs of black beer were sold, and measures of honey, he followed me out of the wild and the wold. He had no thought but to lie over me again, until Gilgamesh descended in gold and myrrh, and paid my temple in silver coin for the taming of Enkidu. Then the eyes of the giant were full of the muscled king, and between them they wrote over my tablets until even my name, first of all his words, had gone into the wet clay and vanished. It was scraped from his tongue and in its place Gilgamesh wrote curses and guilt with his kisses, for no man should have horns more splendid than his own.

This is what was scratched from the tablets of Gilgamesh. I am Genesis; I am the creation of man in the garden-crucible. I am initiation, I am expulsion. But this is not enough - room must be made for the brother-heroes and their quests. Room must be made for the destruction of the world by water, and the cursing of my name by the creature I fashioned on the anvil of my body. Room must be made

She Nailed a Stake Through His Head

for Gilgamesh to love Enkidu. The harlot has only one story,
after all, and the hero has many—why let her into the tale at
all?

     Gilgamesh sprawls—and I disappear.

        (The taming done, I went into the temple
         in the shadow of the cedar slats of the Ishtar Gate.

        I went into the hall where harlots dwell,
        and their perfumes hung in the air
        like banners of victory.

        But the smell of the golem was on me,
        and the sour-milk smell of Gilgamesh.
        My sisters did not know me,
        and they turned from me in fear.
        They saw me and sprang away.

        My knees longed to go among them,
        but they wore only their second bodies to me,
        and would not call me Shamhat again.)

     This was the Last Tablet.

Judgment at Naioth
by Elissa Malcohn

The road to Naioth lay like a razor's edge upon the land, a straight-shot cut into the valley. Some say the road had crested a hilltop before everything had turned inside-out. Others say it was once a river - and then a wadi - and then just a faint line in the desert before the line got paved, one lane in each direction with waves of heat shimmering off the tar. Enough puddle mirages collected to suggest a year's rain, or the hand of God reaching down when the sun climbed high enough to bleach the macadam and melt Route 18 into the sky.

Tamar gunned her Dromedary bike away from the pastel kitsch of downtown Ramah. The black leather on her back soaked up twilight's fading warmth. Wind chill from the East made her cheekbones feel sharper and lifted her short, spiky hair to blend with the encroaching night.

Main Street dropped farther behind, leaving warehouse blocks to either side of 18. The cameras caught Tamar in blips of reflection, a blur streaking across empty sheets. Her engine roar echoed against aluminum siding. Behind the buildings rose mountains; the scars of clear-cut eclipsing the heavens.

In another world, the warehouse called Naioth would have been like any other building, a nondescript blot on the barren landscape, its dented metal dressed in rusted padlocks. To hear the prophets talk, that Naioth existed in that other world. In another world still, it was a moon base, or an abandoned subway tunnel, or a dusty street corner mapped only in repeating dreams. It depended on whom you listened to, if you could untangle the slurred tongues the druggies used to spout their ecstasies. In the end they all said the same thing.

Naioth was the navel of Yahweh.

Tamar listened to them because of the light in their eyes. The light told her that they didn't need the drugs. The remains of their wasted bodies told her they did.

She wheeled her Dromedary into the lot and dismounted. The steel studs on her jacket and pants flashed in the fading light. She passed beneath a tall sign with worn block letters in a round-bulbed frame. Half the bulbs had been burned out for eons. The other half kept shining, as if powered by eternal filaments. Hanging high off the ground and shrouded in perpetual gloaming, they kept the name of NAIOTH visible to those who knew where to look.

Leave it to God to put His navel out in the middle of nowhere.

She laughed. Like anything Yahweh did made sense.

***

Loudspeakers shook with the screams of two dozen steel strings on reverb. A melody hid somewhere in the cacophony, but Tamar couldn't find it. The noise blew through her, as though rending the very fabric of the universe. More likely it was just bad music.

It must have been more than that for the prophet stumbling in the smoky dark, bumping into Tamar and pointing toward empty space.

She hunched over and grumbled into his ear, "I don't see anything, Solomon."

His shaky finger wove. "Look closer, sister."

"I'm not your sister."

She scowled at the malnourished youth, whose rheumy eyes argued, *Yes, you are.*

Tamar raised her voice during an especially painful crescendo. "Trust me, Sol, I've had my fill of half-brothers. That's not a role you want to play." She waved toward a distant stage. "Do you really want that wreck for a father?"

He giggled by her side.

"No choice."

No. Probably not. Tamar shot a glance at Solomon's sallow face and at the sticks that passed for arms and legs. His bony finger kept pointing.

He wore his linen ephod over a threadbare rayon shirt and blue jeans ripped at the knees. Tamar looked away, but Solomon's hand returned her gaze to his vision, whatever it was.

What prophet *didn't* point? For that matter, what prophet *wasn't* related to her? Solomon was probably right about their shared blood, considering all the women who followed David into his trailer between sets, clutching bottles of cheap wine.

In front, hundreds of bodies rubbed against each other like millet in a hopper. They gyrated to the waves of distortion tearing from her father's onyx lyre. Tamar could see only a fuzzy stage glow from the far end of the warehouse. If she squinted, she could make out David's tiny, hyperactive silhouette.

Solomon tried to shout above the din. Tamar hunched down to hear him better.

"He can't open the way," the kid was saying.

"Between the worlds," she said. She'd visited often enough to know the lingo.

Solomon's finger drew a line in the air as he nodded. "Slit's still good and tight."

The lyre's scream intensified as blood roared in Tamar's head. Solomon's choking brought her out of her haze of rage. She hadn't remembered grabbing his pale neck.

She stared at the welts her thumbs left before the boy doubled over, coughing. She rasped down at him, "Very bad choice of words."

He shook his head, tears streaming from his eyes.

Her rape was no great secret, but only Tamar and Amnon had heard that filthy croon. Amnon had not referred to rips in the universe when he sang those words. He'd been too busy ripping into her.

"Did the Mayor of Ramah tell you to say that?" The ephod bunched in Tamar's tapered fingers.

Solomon clutched her arms, wheezing. His head swung side to side. "No. Yahweh…"

She pushed him away. Leave it to the Deity to taunt her. At least Tamar stood too far back to see the panties thrown onstage as her wasted father tortured his instrument.

***

The din faded as Tamar descended to the bar. Her steel-toed boots clanged against Naioth's curved stairs, metal scaffolding cold as a snake's spine.

Her own violence had shaken her. Again. The light of Yahweh might shine from Solomon's eyes, but he was still just a boy. She'd kill him if she wasn't careful.

And the child was blameless. He'd never laid a finger on her. He said what he was told to say; he saw what Yahweh wanted him to see. That's all. If Tamar killed anyone, it should be the Mayor of Ramah. If Yahweh were

68

truly a just god, Amnon would be dead instead of lounging in his City Hall, smug under his cloak of respectability.

She huffed through smoke, passing yellow lamps hanging off the basement's paneled wall. The dark wood complemented the bar's lack of windows, creating a pungent cocoon of drug-laced air. She didn't need to drop extra shekels for hallucinogens in her wine.

Neither did Absalom. Planted at his usual table, his thick mane curled down a backrest as he stared into his drink, looking even more sour than usual. He lifted a heavy head, green eyes meeting Tamar's.

She dropped into the chair opposite his. "Why do I even come here?"

"To get away from him." Absalom's honey-colored eyebrow twitched. "It's either that or move out of Ramah altogether."

"Like you did."

Absalom leaned back and took a long swig from a chipped glass. His white shirt yawned open, letting his muscles catch the light. "Those three years in Geshur taught me that you can't get away from anything. Least of all your fate."

"And your fate is to guzzle wine in Naioth's basement until you pass out."

"I wish." His smooth fingers laced around the glass. "The prophets tell me differently."

Echoes from David's lyre dropped through the ceiling and vanished in a steady buzz of slurred gossip. Absalom stared at the terebinth-paneled walls. Tamar waited.

"Do you want to get rid of Amnon for good?"

Tamar laughed and sipped her wine. She wanted to smash her glass and take its pointed shards to the mayor's balls. She didn't have to repeat her desire to her brother. Absalom had heard her oft-repeated rants over many a drink. "You're telling me it's possible, this time."

"I'm telling you it's necessary, this time." His eyes searched hers out. "But if Amnon dies, then you'll lose me, too."

He had to be pickled. This wasn't the first time Absalom had proposed a suicide mission, planning to storm past the mayor's retinue of security officers and bodyguards. He'd certainly get no sympathy from Ramah's citizens. Amnon had wiped the town clean of its whores and vagrants; most had relocated to cesspools like Geshur.

Tamar tilted her chair back and crossed a studded ankle over her knee.

"So, brother," she murmured, "how do you propose we do the deed this time?"

"We have to kill David."

His voice had never sounded more sober.

***

Three fully-dosed drinks later, Tamar still didn't understand the prophecy. The drugs didn't do anything for her. The alcohol only made her muzzy-headed.

She stood in the parking lot, trying to wash her brain clean in the cold desert air. Meteors streaked above as the Milky Way arced past zenith. Tamar looked away from the black slit of its Great Rift. Nothing but dust obscured the light.

The still-lit bulbs around Naioth's sign seemed brighter, like little supernovas next to dark glass and snapped filaments.

Absalom consulted with Solomon inside. For a place the druggies claimed as the navel of Yahweh, Naioth possessed its share of lint. How many prophets had claimed that their universe - this universe - had been put together all wrong?

In another world, David was king of Israel and Judah, the logical conclusion to his gang wars with the Philistines. He wasn't supposed to be a washed-up rocker dissipating himself on the outskirts of town.

"Why not be a king?" Tamar leaned against a darkened lamppost and chortled, feeling sick. "America has Elvis, no?"

She had long ago given up yearning to kill her father. Watching David's deterioration had faded Tamar's hatred to a slurry of disgusted pity whenever she gazed upon Naioth's hazy stagemaster. Her old man's debts had long ago claimed the spacious ranch house where she'd been forced to live with Amnon. She'd spent her childhood trying to hide as her half-brother's lust tracked her from every corner.

Tamar wasn't about to begrudge David his inevitable decline, or his cramped trailer reeking of stale beer and staler sex.

He wasn't the one in power.

You're wrong. The memory of Solomon's thin voice sliced through the dark. The boy had looked like a wraith beside Absalom's robust, cut build. *Everything hinges on Father.*

The vision seemed ludicrous and cruel, but Tamar was no prophet. Worse, if David died to set the universe right, it wouldn't erase what Amnon had done.

That part of the prophecy doesn't change, Tamar.

71

She turned watery eyes to the stars. She might be scarred in her agony, but she was alive. If Solomon spoke for Yahweh, then a repaired universe demanded Absalom's death as well.

Tamar tried to glimpse the vast family gathered in Solomon's vision. For a time even the metallic screams of David's lyre faded behind a bleating chorus of sheep. The smells of wool and roasted mutton overpowered Naioth's acrid smoke. The dancers pressing against the stage became princes lounging in a sunny oasis. Jasmine-scented breezes raised the corners of festive tents.

They'd all become creatures of antiquity. Decked in finery, Absalom whispered to his attendants. A drunken Amnon sprawled beneath peacock feather fans waved by servants. When he nodded off, the attendants followed their master's instructions, the first in line slipping a swift blade between the prince rapist's ribs.

The universe around that too-quick, too-merciful execution doomed Absalom, too. He also had to die, so that David's forty-year reign could change the world.

Tamar's steel toe scraped against gravel.

Tell me, Yahweh, how is the world better for that?

No heavenly voice or prophetic whisper answered. Meteors sporadic continued burning themselves out. What did she expect from God? She wasn't the visionary.

If Saul were alive, Naioth might not even exist to house wasted prophets spouting their drivel. Tamar almost wished for a return to the incessant raids, which had increased in intensity and frequency after her father had fled Naioth in the first place. If Naioth were gone, maybe she could leave Ramah behind, never mind Absalom's mutterings about fate.

For what would fate be without the prophecies?

Judgment at Naioth by Elissa Malcohn

The prophets are addicted to the drugs, and you're addicted to the prophets. She barked a laugh. For all its destitution, this wretched outpost held more truth than pretty Ramah's tourist jitneys and picture postcards and deed restrictions. Filth lurked behind the fresh water spat from Ramah's marble fountains, behind its shopkeepers flashing pearly teeth. Clean streets. A complacent populace. Tamar wondered how many maidens Amnon banged each day, squeaking the black leather on his executive couch.

He owned the apartment complex to which she would return before dawn. Nothing could stop him from procuring a key and letting himself in. She *should* have left Ramah.

***

"I would stop him, Tamar."

She shifted uneasily on her chair in Ramah's precinct office, squinting against the desert sun pouring past slatted blinds. Her cotton-covered knees pressed tightly together.

"I doubt that, Jonathan. You're on Amnon's payroll."

The chief of police steepled his fingers above a busy desk. A fan fluttered dispatches tacked to the wall as his gray eyes scrutinized her. "I share your concern for safety, Tamar. Let me remind you again that my surveillance costs for your building come out of my own pocket, not that it matters. I'm not trying to buy your trust."

"I don't trust easily."

"Nor should you." Jonathan smoothed down his salt-and-pepper goatee. "But that's not why you're here, is it? You usually come to me in the spring with this complaint."

Tamar twisted in her chair. Maybe the sunlight would burn clarity into her if she stared at the window long enough. "Solomon told me to see you."

"Bathsheba's boy?" He reached for a manila folder. "Is his mother in trouble again?"

"No, nothing like that."

His gnarled hands flipped through pages.

"It isn't like a prophet to contact the police, even through an intermediary. You know the deal, Tamar. I leave the prophets alone and they leave me alone. You can thank Amnon for that. If Saul were still mayor, it'd be a different story."

Tamar blinked afterimages away. She looked back at Jonathan's pinched brow, at his fingers nestled in graying locks. The chief of police still had his own issues. "Amnon's my father's firstborn son, but that isn't the only reason why you leave Naioth alone."

"We're not here to talk about me, Tamar, or about David. What do you want?"

"I *am* here to talk about David."

Jonathan looked up from his papers.

"He's supposed to be a king. Solomon said."

"That's because the boy still loves his father." His chair tilted back on well-oiled hinges. "I can't say that I blame him. You've got a drugged child hero-worshipping a man who remains larger than life. I don't doubt David is the king of Naioth, and he will *be* the king of Naioth until he dies. Beloved by the lascivious and the insane."

His long sigh stretched across the room.

"We can let them both be happy."

"David's not supposed to be like this."

"Do you think I don't know that? I loved your father, Tamar."

74

"That's not what I mean. The word of Yahweh..."

Jonathan's eyes flashed. Tamar stopped speaking.

"What the hell has the word of Yahweh got to do with a dilapidated dance club? That's not religion, Tamar. It's the drug trade. It's the black marketers. Burn out enough brain cells and you'd speak in ecstasy, too."

He tossed the folder aside. His argument sounded forced, as if he didn't believe himself. "There is nothing sacred about putting on an ephod and falling down in your own piss."

How readily she wanted to agree - to ignore the light in Solomon's eyes as they offered visions before her like a perverse movie projector. If her mission succeeded, Jonathan would also die beheaded on Mount Gilboa, impaled on the wall at Beth-shan, cremated in Jabesh. Shattered bones buried under a tamarisk tree.

She whispered, "Solomon told me I would hear the word of God in the room of Michal's bride price."

The sudden terror in Jonathan's eyes made her want to flee. Tamar huddled in her thin blouse; waited as he rubbed circulation back into his hands. She watched the fan make its slow rotations. A gust toyed with her spiky hair. Then it turned back toward the papers, a soft whir fading beneath Jonathan's labored breaths.

"David delivered that bride price to my father," the chief of police said. "My father set up that room and then bequeathed it to me. No one else - certainly no woman - has ever set foot inside it or has even known of its existence. Not even David knew what became of Michal's bride price."

Tamar didn't have to tell him that Yahweh had spoken of it first, squirting the drops of knowledge into Solomon's addled brain. She didn't have to tell Jonathan that Naioth was more than a dive. He'd been there, leading dozens of raids during Saul's pursuit of her father. Despite his protests, the chief of police knew that Yahweh had everything to do with the dilapidated dance club that had finally taken David away. The vein throbbed at Jonathan's temple.

She struggled to find her voice. "I tell you only what Solomon told me."

The papers on the wall lost their animation as Jonathan switched off the fan. Shadows fattened when he shut the blinds.

"Amnon won't have access to your living quarters." He steered Tamar toward the door. His scowl almost hid his distress. "You're moving in with me."

"I wasn't thinking…"

"No, Tamar, you weren't. You don't know what you ask of me, but God does. And if you are to be His instrument, then it is my job to protect you."

"The way you couldn't protect my father."

Jonathan tightened his grip on her elbow and said nothing. She stumbled by his side. The buttons on his uniform gleamed as they stepped into the sunlight.

***

She didn't have much to move. Tamar's mother Maacah hadn't left much to her and Absalom, just enough to get by in the likes of Ramah. The shekels behaved differently at Naioth, materializing and multiplying in emptied-out pockets and leaving enough odd bits of change to procure a meal or a drink when needed, or a chemical cocktail when desperate. Money changed hands among unseen forces in Naioth. Maybe Yahweh just enjoyed being a pickpocket in reverse.

76

Tamar's hairs stood on the back of her neck as she towed her belongings past City Hall. She didn't have to look up to know Amnon stood before the third-floor window, watching her Dromedary's slow passage. Nothing got by David's eldest.

Beside her, Jonathan said, "I won't let him touch you."

She whispered, "Too late."

Whoever lay spread-eagled on the mayor's couch couldn't be half as fun as the terrified adolescent of old.

Jonathan added, "I won't touch you, either."

"You could lose your job for taking me in."

"I won't."

Tamar assumed Jonathan's answer was more an issue of faith than politics. A nervous laugh bubbled up her throat. What would the chief of police say if he knew she'd been told to kill David and destroy the world? This twisted universe was the only one Tamar knew. Who was to say a better one existed?

Yahweh.

If Yahweh was so damned powerful, then why didn't He do His own housecleaning? Abraham's arguments with God must have set a sick precedent for collaboration. Humans were very adept at doing His dirty work, not to mention their own.

"I hate prophets," she growled.

Jonathan nodded.

"So do I."

Jonathan's properties lay in Ramah's historic district, close to Samuel's former digs. Tamar took some comfort in knowing that the chief of police lived in better quarters than the mayor. Tamar pulled her belongings up narrow streets, swerving past the occasional pothole. City Hall's gilded cupola shone below in late afternoon light.

Rumpled and sweaty from the climb, she parked her Dromedary and trailer just outside a high cast-iron gate. They waited for the old mansion's locks to release. Twilight peeked around turrets and Jonathan's grandson Micah buzzed them in.

Even within the safety of his own home, Jonathan stood guard outside the door to the bath. Tamar performed her ritual purifications in the mikvah, trying not to garble her prayers. How did one pray when given divine license to commit patricide?

So that David can live as he is supposed to live.

Maybe Absalom wouldn't have to die in the repaired universe. Maybe Jonathan could live as well, serving at his king's side. Solomon's visions could be wrong, couldn't they? Yahweh could change His mind, couldn't He? After all, He'd struck bargains in the past. With Abraham. With Lot.

God doesn't change His mind.

So Samuel had told Jonathan's father Saul, who had known that hard truth better than anyone. David had recounted that story in one of his more lucid moments. Tamar's father then added, "Unless, of course, He decides otherwise."

She shivered as her water cooled. Asking the Deity for favors would do her no good. She'd been sent here to gather the strength she needed to open the fabric of creation. To accomplish what her father's tortured strumming could not.

She dried off, pulled on a green silk robe, and padded after Jonathan. The mansion's fragrant hall ribboned down a straightaway. Guest rooms dropped behind. Plush carpets receded and left a blank stone floor in their wake as the air turned musty. Crudely-hacked stairs marked the entrance to the farthest turret, nowhere left to go but up.

Jonathan lifted an old lantern off its hook and struck a match.

"No electricity upstairs?" said Tamar.

"No."

She heard the hoarseness in his voice. His harsh look silenced her. Exaggerated shadows preceded them up the stairway's tight coil. They climbed single-file. Without a railing for support, Tamar braced her palms against curved walls, her bare soles clammy. The stone steps swallowed Jonathan's footfalls.

One moment she wondered if the bride price for Michal was a treasure locked away, like a fairy tale princess imprisoned in a high tower. The next moment it struck her as a holy of holies, fit to be seen only by priests.

She whispered, "What's in the room?"

Jonathan paused in his long climb for a moment. Then he shook his head and pressed on.

A narrow slit in the turret's thick wall afforded a bird's eye view of Route 18. The straight-edge road dwindled to its vanishing point in the night. The black silhouettes of mountains blotted out the horizon. If Tamar looked hard enough, she could see the lights of Naioth, distant and fuzzy like a nebula.

Why me?

Solomon's answer rang in her head.

Because you know what it is to be sacrificed.

And that gave her the right to sacrifice others? Tamar gritted her teeth, wrenched herself away from the view and followed Jonathan. He had reached the landing and pushed an ancient skeleton key into a lock. Gears tumbled, sounding deceptively well-oiled.

He murmured, "My father had asked for one hundred. David gave him twice that."

The heavy oak door eased open and warm air enveloped them in a sickening blast. Tamar reeled from musk as the police chief's arm came around her waist.

At first glance the shriveled brown lumps looked like roaches. Then Jonathan raised his lamp. Tamar made out the shapes impaled on the rounded wall.

"Philistine foreskins." He spoke in a flat voice.

They studded the plaster, curling in on themselves like little fists. Nail heads reflected the lamp light.

Only her thin silk robe separated Tamar's nakedness from the cobbled room's treasure. She clutched Jonathan's jacket, trying not to throw up. "Saul was a madman."

"Wasn't he?"

Another tilt of the lamp and the nails shone like eyes out of wrinkled sockets.

"But even madmen know what they're doing."

Was he talking about his father or about Naioth? Tamar couldn't tell. Bathsheba's boy must have been mad himself, to send her to this place. Saul himself had been no stranger to the dance club.

She started to giggle and couldn't stop. Why end at foreskins? Why not enact the entire castration fantasy, her desired fate for Amnon writ large? Had the Philistines been circumcised before or after they'd been killed? Why limit oneself to just a single act of pain? Cold sweat ran into her eyes. Tamar doubled over, blowing dry heaves.

"You didn't know what Ramah was like before David drove the Philistines away." Jonathan's voice took on a dreamy tone as his warm hands held her shoulders. "They

80

spilled in from the coast. Their seranim bosses ran this town and every single outpost and oasis up and down Route 18. You saw their colors on every street corner. You heard their revved-up Dromedaries day and night."

His words fell to a whisper. "Amnon was righteous compared to them. My sister Michal's rage lives in this room because of what they'd done to her. She didn't bear your father or anyone else any children, because she couldn't."

The chief of police fell silent. Tamar eased her hold on his sleeve and sank to her knees. The cold floor ferried chills up her spine.

"The Philistines learned to be subtle after that, Tamar. They learned to be patient, and that's how they exacted their revenge on David. Through my father, and through Naioth."

What a fool she'd been, to believe the club drugs could have come from God. Who peddled the wine? Who struck the secret deals in Naioth's dark corners? Who couriered mysterious packages back and forth, to Gath and Ekron, then west to the sea, to Ashdod and Ashkelon and Gaza?

She choked, "Not the navel of Yahweh, after all."

Jonathan knelt beside her.

"Except that it is, Tamar. That much about Naioth is true, but you'll never hear me admit it in public. There's too much at stake. My father had ordered all of our priests killed, but he couldn't touch the prophets. They remain active at Naioth, where God keeps them alive and the Philistines keep them addicted. David's dependence is only part of the reason he's never left that place. That awful music he plays is the only form of prayer he's got left and it keeps the prophets by him. Believe me, Tamar, he is still battling the Philistines."

81

Her eyes couldn't turn away from the helpless foreskins. "Solomon said I knew what it was to be sacrificed."

Jonathan nodded.

"So does your father."

***

Solomon's instructions had been clear. Tamar caught Jonathan's wavering gaze, as he locked her in. She listened to the click of his skeleton key and then his muffled footfalls as he descended.

She could still smell the room's pungencies. How much fresh air remained before she suffocated, trembling on a stone floor in pitch blackness, frozen and blind? She certainly couldn't have picked a better spot to hide from Amnon. Compared to her current terror, the Mayor of Ramah faded into a blip of creation.

"Solomon said you'd speak to me, Yahweh." Tamar hugged her breasts, teeth chattering. "I'm listening."

Two hundred nail heads watched her. Tamar craned her neck, blinking. Where was the point source for the light? Michal's bride-price room held no windows. No moon cast its illumination. No planets. No stars. Nothing to reflect.

Heady warmth climbed the rounded wall; circles formed around the metal eyes. Soft colors at first, half hidden. A muted orange sheen spread across the floor, illuming Tamar's naked feet, brightening her muscled calves before touching the hem of her robe. Rings of dead foreskin began to glow like embers. They continued to burn, unconsumed.

Tamar held her breath as they uncrumpled; they stretched forth from their nails, supple and elongated, edges flaring. Heat blew through their stretched membranes. They emitted a sound that began as a gentle whistling, like wind through trees; then the song took on an urgency like a harp abandoned on a hilltop, all of its strings alive at once. A prelude to the horns.

She jerked as the circumcised mouths opened wide and released a sudden blast that shook the wall. Tamar squeezed her palms between her knees to keep from covering her ears. Every bone in her body shook, but she had come to *listen*. The dismemberments trumpeted, waving at her like wild anemones.

If she shut her eyes, all she heard was triumph. Empty shells, swelled and proud. Tamar forced herself to watch, chiding herself for being naïve enough to have expected *words*.

Nothing surrounded her but sonorous charges of dead air. The annunciation of a mirage. Two hundred hoods slit from the shaft, the world pulled inside-out with a scream.

The foreskins gained in length, twisting as though threaded on a spindle. They curled and thickened, honey-colored now, silken. Tangled in a terebinth branch in the forest of Ephraim.

Absalom's corpse hung before his sister, his green eyes dulled. Drowning in a pool of orange light, Tamar beat her breast and wailed.

By morning the pool had deepened in color and stuck to her thighs, turning Michal's bride price room into Tamar's red tent. Seven days she bled onto the floor. Seven nights the foreskins roared. Tamar dreamed of berry bushes. She ran through the woods of Ephraim, awakening with purpled fingers and sweetness on her tongue.

She Nailed a Stake Through His Head

The bride price taught her that nothing mattered. Civilizations rose and fell. Scriptures twisted. Promised lands fell to dust. Freak rains buried sand dunes in overgrowth. She believed what she wanted to believe, and everything mattered then.

Her flow abated as the foreskins shriveled like fruits left too long on the vine. Tamar awoke to a door cracking open and the sight of Jonathan's back. Her stained robe dragged on the floor as she followed him. She kept her distance for as long as it took to reach the mikvah.

***

Her Dromedary shrieked across the desert. Some day Tamar would ride Route 18 to its end and skid off the cosmic edge, flying like a stone from a sling.

Today, she had a world to destroy.

Her boots touched gravel as she swerved into the lot. Naioth's strobes turned her jacket and pants to sparkles. She stepped inside the warehouse. The mosh pit continued to writhe, a single organism beside a murky stage.

Absalom stood next to her, studying the knife in his hands.

"At least I'll win the hearts of Israel," he mused. "For a time."

Tamar didn't question how she heard him through the din. She slipped her arm around his waist. Give her a grip on the blade, give her one moment, and she could shear him. Neutralize the instrument of his death.

But that leonine mane grew back. Year after year, cut after cut. Two hundred shekels of weight on which to hang.

Absalom passed her the onyx handle. Her green eyes glowed, reflected in tempered steel.

"I'm ready." He gave Tamar's shoulder a last squeeze and faced toward the stage. "Help him."

The knife slid into her boot. Clad in black leather, Tamar ducked between warehouse struts and glided forward, a slick skimming the walls. She skirted the seranim bosses in shadow and averted her eyes from narcotics changing hands. The prophets phosphoresced in her sight now. She tracked them like a trail of bread crumbs to the stage.

Their rags whirled to her left and right, before and behind her. Asahel and Elhanan, Mahrai and Sibbecai. Heled. Eleazar. Lunatic warriors. Japhia palming a handful of pills. Nathan injecting a vein.

Wedged behind a speaker, Bathsheba's boy huddled slack-jawed in mid-high, his eyes unfocused. Tamar eased tender fingers against Solomon's curls and moved on.

The closer she got to the music, the more Naioth shimmered like the surface of a lake. Reality rippled around her, ready to part like the Reed Sea one moment and slamming shut the next. Then it turned deceptively solid, a meniscus held together by the surface tension of faith.

The black wood of David's lyre called to the black wood in her boot, vibrating her handle along the grain.

Forgive me, Jonathan.

The lyre's dissonance strangled the air. Tamar gazed upon twitching limbs, then at David's blistered and bleeding fingers. She glanced back at the moshers sweating under hot lights, stripped concubines working their poles.

Someone pressed a vial into her hand. She almost smashed it against the ground, but its gelcaps weren't drugs. Bathsheba's boy managed a dazed smile before he turned away.

The universe cracked, and the blast from a thousand ram's horns hurled Tamar onto the stage before the crack mended. When it did, she looked into the face of an old man with sallow cheeks and dark circles under his eyes. David swayed before her, exhausted, his flesh and muscle melted away.

He whispered through flaking lips, "Quickly."

Tamar spilled the gelcaps into her hand and made a fist above his head. Oil spurted from between her fingers.

"I anoint you, Father."

Seranim reflected in his eyes. Out of the shadows now, reaching into their vests.

Tamar bent to grab the handle and drove her blade upward as the shots rang out.

***

"You seem distracted, Aunt."

Smoke curled up from a distant forge. Tamar listened to the far-off hammer and clang of carpenters and smiths, a quiet prelude to the explosion of industry to come. The 80,000 quarriers alone would make enough noise to rend creation. "Wouldn't you be?"

"I suppose."

"This won't be an ordinary house, you know."

Her niece's chin dimpled as she grinned. Tamar's young namesake had grown into a beautiful woman. Absalom's daughter. The dimple came from her mother, but her eyes were his.

After a life lived from tent to tent, the Ark of the Covenant was finally coming home. The thought of Yahweh readying to settle down sounded more blasphemous than it felt. Considering God in such familiar terms would certainly invite disaster if spoken aloud.

Would it? Tamar had to admit to herself that she wasn't really sure, but it was probably safe to remain silent. At times like these she existed apart from the others, even within the boisterous throngs of Solomon's court. She'd never settled fully into the world. Was it any wonder she felt an odd and abiding bond with the Ineffable?

All the sweet-smelling wood to come, the cedar and cypress and algum dressed in gold and bronze - all of the precious stones, all the purple and blue and crimson yarns, all the engravings - if those could satisfy the Deity, then what was her complaint? The sheer size of the Temple would anchor the world in place.

Such a structure must endure forever, no?

If existence were solid. In Tamar's dreams existence ran like water. Like sand. She couldn't explain.

Passing clouds stretched their fingers, making daylight play on Mount Moriah. Tamar and her niece followed their changing forms as the younger woman sighed in admiration. Perhaps the shadows delineated the Temple's rooms and porches to its upper chambers and inner chambers. Perhaps they matched the blueprints that the new king consulted, before the clouds that cast them vanished into blue or fell as rain.

For Tamar, the future cut a razor's edge upon a land with no vanishing point.

But the land was filled with dunes. And the dunes always shifted.

Judith & Holofernes
by Romie Stott

Judith didn't know how many times she'd beheaded Holofernes. Counting skulls didn't cut it - too many given away as souvenirs, or repurposed as building material. Bone is stronger than tent; that's a fact.

The first time, she begged to do it. Her husband was dead, and there wasn't much to occupy her time. She felt patriotic about the whole thing. Seduce the enemy general, drink lots of wine, go back to his room, and off him. A one time deal. If she died, well, she died. That was war.

Only she didn't die, and he didn't either, and the constant beheading became a full time job.

Holofernes asked for a massage. Judith knelt on his back as he lay on his stomach. She placed a knife at his throat and leaned backward. The advantage of this position was arterial spray. The blood would flow away from her, due both to gravity and the position of the cut. Judith imitated a kosher butcher: sawing indifferently, careful not to apply too much force as she cut toward herself.

Judith showed the head to her maid. It was still attached to Holofernes. "Would you look at this head," said Judith, rubbing Holofernes' temple with her thumb. The maid leaned in for a closer look.

"What are you doing?" asked Holofernes.

"I do this not for myself, but for my people," said Judith.

Holofernes wore a gold torc, which made for a nice guide rail. Judith was confused, but trusting. She slid the sword along the torc and it was like cutting through butter. Holofernes made a lot of noise as he bled out onto the pillow; which Judith found distasteful. Her maid waited with a sack, unsure what to do with her hands.

Judith stole Holofernes' sword. It was like a long dagger, or perhaps a short scimitar. Her maid seemed to wear a crown. The curls of Holofernes' hair matched pleasingly with the folds of draped canvas.

Holofernes knelt at Judith's feet, head buried between her legs. With great moral certainty, she turned his tongue from its business and held his face to her thigh. She lifted a sword over her head, and as he turned to look, her hand tangled in his hair.

Holofernes was a dirty old man. When he slept, he lay on his back and threw his arms out to take up the whole bed. Judith, as always, took the time to dress. Her maid helped her put pearls in her hair. The two went through Holofernes' large collection of swords and settled on an elaborately engraved number with only one sharp side. This reminded them of both jewelry and kitchen knives. Judith picked a bad angle for her first hack, and sliced through Holofernes' jaw and into his mouth. As he gurgled, she calmly struck again. Her maid patted her shoulder comfortingly.

Judith stuck her fingers in Holofernes' mouth. She carefully drew a dotted line across his neck with a pencil. He was frightened, but froze half-in, half-out of bed, stunned by the sudden appearance of several fat cupids.

Judith wore a large hat. Holofernes' head, once removed, was an empty sock. "Oh Holofernes," Judith seemed to say. She cast her eyes down and to the left, coyly.

Judith's maid held the head on a metal tray, which she balanced on her own head. Holofernes' head was giant, easily the size of a roast turkey. Judith hurried to cover it as they raced down the hall.

Judith & Holofernes by Romie Stott

Judith leaned against the broadsword, foot playfully resting atop Holofernes' head. She rolled it back and forth along ball and arch. She wondered absently whether she could pick the head up with her toes, but it was heavy. She couldn't decide whether to grab the hair or pinch the nose.

Judith's maid held Holofernes down. She shouldn't have been able to; he was a strong man. In his drunken flailing, he practically cut his own throat. Everything looked distorted - arms too big for bodies and heads ending at the hairline. Judith felt ugly - mannish - disgusted.

Judith brought a manservant. He efficiently wrapped and removed the head, and Judith returned to entertaining on the harpsichord.

Judith held a hand against the candlelight, and waited to let her eyes adjust to the darkness. Her maid knelt beside her, grabbing whatever rags she could find to wipe up the blood.

"You're not the maid here," joked Judith.

"Don't hold that sword so close to me," said the maid.

Afterward, Judith wore a triumphant smile; always, she was applauded. Once Holofernes' head was off, he looked nothing like Holofernes. His body looked not like a man's body, but like a plucked chicken, silly and a little embarrassing.

Judith took the prettiest heads on lecture tours. To these events, which inevitably sold out, she wore thick gold collars to emphasize the place where head usually met neck. She had dreams in which armies poured from Nebuchadnezzar's mouth. On good nights, she woke when Holofernes was still a lump in Nebuchadnezzar's throat. On most nights, he smiled as he worked past the jaws.

She Nailed a Stake Through His Head

Sometimes Judith dreamed that after she beheaded Holofernes, Nebuchadnezzar poured out of his neck.

Judith didn't know how many times she'd beheaded Holofernes, but her husband stayed dead. He never came back. Not even once. She wrote some songs about it, and about the Lord, but they didn't help much.

Jawbone of an Ass
by Lyda Morehouse

The first thing most people notice about my husband is his hair. It's huge. He has tight crazy-curls, and it grows out, like a bad clown wig, despite his black Irish complexion. Then, most red-blooded women (and blue-blooded boys) tend to let their gaze linger on those bulging muscles. The neighbor ladies all peer at me jealously from behind lace curtains. They think I've found a real catch in Michael Morrison, hero of the Irish cause. I know better. Because, for me, it's his eyes that always hit me first. God, I've come to believe, lives in those eyes, and God hates me.

Morrison's pupils should be unremarkable; his irises are dark and the shape of them kind of on the piggish side. Yet, even as he glances between the tellie and window, I wince in those few seconds his gaze lights upon me on the way to more important things. I feel their holy fire like a brand: burning me, setting my cheeks ablaze in a blush that sears my very center.

My husband isn't looking at me yet, despite the fact that I'm standing mere inches away from the table where he sits reading the *Irish Times*. I've been standing here for a few minutes trying to get up my courage to speak. I wouldn't even attempt to bridge the chasm between us, if it wasn't for my parents. Londonderry could burn with my husband's wrath, for all I care. But my parents want the answer to his riddle or they will turn me into the SAS, the British Special Forces, for harboring a criminal.

It's a ridiculous charge since I am, after all, married to the man, but they have governmental strings to pull and I know my father could make the charge stick. Plus, my parents know where I live, and the SAS would never think to find Morrison here, in the "lace curtain" Protestant neighborhood of Londonderry. Moreover, even if they did, this is not the part of town one randomly raids. It's simply not done.

I shift my feet. His eyes continue to scan the newsprint in front of him. His face crumples with intensity, like Rodin's philosopher, but from where I'm standing I can see he's reading the sports pages. A brain trust, my lover is not.

Lover is, perhaps, too strong a word. I'm not sure Morrison has ever felt anything for me in all eighteen months of marriage, not even lust. To this day I'm baffled as to why he chose to marry me. He and his soldiers just happened to be walking though the courtyard of my father's estate on their way back to the dockyards. The spring morning was unnaturally warm, and mist formed along the riverbanks. The sun and the fresh tang of earth in the air after such a long, hard winter compelled me out of doors. The song of a lark caught my attention, and, by chance, our eyes met over the garden fence. He stopped like he'd hit an invisible wall. His men continued a few paces before they noticed their commander transfixed, presumably, by the vision of me in my dirty gardening overalls and wide-brimmed straw hat. At first I didn't recognize him; I'd fallen too deeply into those bottomless black eyes.

"She's the one for me," he said slowly, deliberately, almost as if the words were foreign to him and spoken through his mouth by another.

His words broke the spell. Like waking from a dream, I suddenly saw the emblem of the harp on his chest, recognized the gray-green uniform of his men, and realized they were Provos - Provisional I.R.A. More than that, he was the infamous Michael Morrison who, according to legend, single-handedly defeated an entire battalion of British soldiers on the Bogside, knocking down the ghetto walls with his bare hands. Seeing him, I was too shocked to run. His men, too, seemed stunned.

"Are you mad, man?" One of them said, "She's British!"

"I will marry her," Morrison said, his voice still measured in that strange, singsong tone.

Though my face was pale with fear, secretly I felt flattered. He was a legendary outlaw, the kind of rogue-hero you might read about in a romance novel. My parents would be horrified. They might even disown me. That too gave me no little thrill; especially as my father delighted in telling me I had a face like a horse, the kind only a monarch could love. In fact, my father had been desperately courting the favors of a certain young Windsor, a third or fifth cousin to the Queen, whom I found unbearably boorish. Not like this man. This ruffian standing in front of me was a wild, untamable thing, like the tight curls of his hair.

I no longer remember the whirlwind courtship, such as it was, only the bomb threats from both sides, the angry shouts of my father, and the bitter tears wept by my mother. Tears I later shed myself on our wedding night when whatever passions possessing Morrison to pursue me withered. Since then, I have been little more than another piece of furniture occupying space in our Londonderry home.

I clear my throat. Morrison continues studying the football scores, as though they held the same truths as Payne's *Rights of Man*.

"About the riddle you posed the other night," I say.

"Hmmm?" His eyes stay on the page.

"I was just curious," I say, trying to sound light, "what the answer was."

He looks up, revealing his face underneath the helmet of curls. Those black eyes pierce me as though they can see through my calm façade to the hammering beat of my heart.

"Why do you want to know?" Despite myself, I still love his voice. He has a deep Connaught brogue that always seems whiskey-scratched and mellowed.

To lie I have to look away, towards the window and the rain. "I puzzled at it all last night, and it's driving me right mad."

"Truly." He seems unimpressed.

"Really, darling," I tell the curtains, "you are my husband. I hate being left out of the secret."

I sneak a glance at him and see his eyebrow raise, as if to inquire why he should care. That's when I start crying.

"Now what's all this?" He sounds more annoyed than concerned.

My therapist warned me things like this would happen. She explained that my feelings were bollixed up thanks to the pressure of living with such a man as Morrison and being torn between him and my kin.

I can't stop the angry words from tumbling out of my mouth. "You never gave a damn about me, did you? I'm just part of some scheme! Like that crazy riddle of yours!"

My words come out between great gasps of sobs. I hate myself for my weakness, but I can't help it. I still want him. Never once has he touched me, not even a cuff in anger. On our wedding day, when the priest named us man and wife, the skin of his lips grazed mine, feather-light, almost not at all. Now, just like then, my body shakes with unrequited desire.

I crumple into a kitchen table chair, and lay my head down on the cool oak and let the tears pour out. My therapist would say it is wonderfully cathartic, but I couldn't stop if I wanted to. If only the damned Finnian bastard believed in divorce, I curse under my breath. It's a lie, of course. What I want is just the opposite. I love being a rebel's wife, and more, I love being this particular man's wife. Despite myself, his crimes and sedition against Britain cause me to swell with pride and twist with shame.

"All right, love. I'll tell you."

Raising my head from my arms, I blink. "What?"

"If it bothers you so much, I'll tell you." His eyes are soft, like his brogue, and almost kind.

"You will?"

"Dry your tears." He hands me the kerchief from his pocket. As I take it, the very tips of our fingers touch. Breath leaves my chest in a huff. I feel as if someone has hit me hard, right in the solar plexus. He looks up, and our eyes meet, just as they did over the garden gate.

This time, however, I'm not too stunned to see it happen. Something possesses him, or, perhaps, it is the much-whispered-about "Spirit of the Lord" coming mightily upon him. His body shifts as if someone is settling into him as you would a sofa. He looks around our tiny kitchen. His gaze sweeps the lace curtains covering the rain-streaked windows, the dust motes and crumbs in the corner under the stove and the teapot on the counter next to the unwashed dishes. Once oriented, he turns back to look at me.

Morrison's face is transformed. He looks softer, younger and almost...angelic. Yet this thing that watches me is not like the cherubs painted on the chapel ceiling. Instead, it is the kind of angel that wields a flaming sword, and I am the dragon it stands ready to smite.

At that thought, I back away so fast that the chair topples, nearly bringing me down with it. "Who are you?"

"I am who am," it says with a smile unearthly in its joy.

I recognize that answer and it chills me. When it speaks again, I see words form at the same time in a strange script glowing in the space above my husband's head. The symbols form from right to left, and leave burning trails, like the flight of a firefly or swirls of a Guy Fawkes Day sparkler.

There is no doubt in my mind that this is the word of God.

"Do you understand?" It says, speaking in English without my husband's customary brogue.

Strangely, I do. Though the answer makes less sense than my husband's riddle. I nod meekly.

My husband's face beams radiantly.

I am pulling at the wet handkerchief in my hand. As I look down at it, anger, as if stealing flame from the burning bush, sparks in me.

"That I am given the answer can only mean I'm destined to tell it. What if I refuse?"

It blinks my husband's eyes, clearly uncertain what I mean.

I take a shuddering breath. "His plans don't include me, do they? Even Judas got a kiss for his trouble."

It flees. I can see it move through Morrison's body, rippling like wind across water. Then, Morrison yawns and stretches his arms above his head until his shoulders pop.

Picking up the paper, he goes back to the sports and ignoring me.

***

The Royal Ulster Constabulary doesn't seem as surprised as I am when I stumble into the police station. I am out of breath, having run all the way up the hill from our house. The rain trickles down my back where it dribbles off my plastic kerchief.

The officer whose desk I am panting in front of takes one look at me and picks up the phone. "She's here."

He nods a few times in response to the voice on the other end, his posture straightening until I swear he'll salute instead of replacing the receiver in the cradle.

"You can sit there, ma'am." The officer's accent is pure Belfast, hard and nasal. As I look at his auburn crewcut, I think that if my husband had an accent like that I would have betrayed him long ago.

I sink into the chair he's offered, and set my purse on my knees. The police station is little more than a storefront. Desks and battered chairs are strewn around the space with such cluttered carelessness that I would have thought it a thrift store instead of a police station. I sit next to a large window. Sheets of rain patter against it in time with the clacking of someone's keyboard. Through the glass I can see brick row houses in the Catholic area, below. On the side of the walls someone has painted bright white letters which read: "You are now entering Free Derry."

I sneer. It disgusts me that my father thinks of me as one of them: the dirty, rebellious Catholics. So much so that he is willing to send me to jail as a political dissident if I don't tell these policemen the answer to Morrison's riddle.

99

Yet, I have to admit to myself the truth. My father's threats may have compelled me to ask, but it is my spite for God that pushes me onward. That God has chosen sides in this dirtiest of holy wars angers me beyond words.

"Damned bastard," I say under my breath.

"Our thoughts precisely, dear." A crisp Oxford accent says, thinking I'm speaking of Morrison and not his maker.

I look up, expecting to see a suit coat attached to the voice, but am surprised by a black commando military uniform, complete with side arm and the letters SAS on his breast pocket. He smiles when he sees me and the corners of his eyes crinkle, reminding me, in a surprisingly pleasant way, of my father. "Mrs. Morrison, I presume?"

"I have the answer you're looking for," I say awkwardly without preamble.

"Yes, yes," he says taking my hand. His palm is soft and smooth - a gentleman's hand. "Let's talk about it like civilized people, shall we? Over tea."

Tucking my arm through his, he leads me past the tangle of mis-matched furniture to a closet door.

"My office," he explains with an embarrassed smile. An opened door reveals a desk and two chairs. Though the space is cramped, it is lovingly decorated. A framed poster of something by Matisse hangs on the wall, and a pathetic, if well-groomed, potted plant sits at the edge of the small desk. The tiny space is infused with the robust smell of tea.

"Milk?" The SAS officer asks, stepping over the desk to retrieve a carton from a half-refrigerator tucked under the desk.

"Please, thank you," I say, taking the seat opposite him. I am not sure if I should close the door, but someone outside pushes it shut, leaving just a crack open for air.

"I am Captain Andy Braithwaite." He hands me a steaming mug, with another soft smile. "Now, dear, you said you had something for me?"

"I..." I'm here, aren't I? I should just be able to spit it out.

Captain Braithwaite leans in on his elbows and gives me a measuring look. "Mrs. Morrison, you know that if we don't get to the bottom of this, lives are at stake. British lives. Your husband, on the other hand, has agreed to turn over a cache of weapons if we can figure this damned thing out."

The closet walls feel too close. I take a gulp of tea and scald my tongue. Fate curls around me like a shroud, squeezing the breath from my chest.

"Mrs. Morrison?"

"I..." I honestly intend to deny it all. I want to say it has all been a mistake my coming here, that really, despite angelic possession and neglect, I love my husband and am a good wife. Instead, I tell the Captain what he wants.

"It is Samson's riddle to the Philistines, Judges 14:18," I explain. "'What is sweeter than honey? And what is stronger than a lion? Out of the eater came forth the meat, and out of the strong came forth sweetness.'"

"Clever bastard using the Bible like that," Braithwaite says, scribbling my words onto the blotter under his keyboard.

I raise an eyebrow, but can not speak. If only he knew which clever bastard is really waging war against him, against us all - the modern Philistines.

I leave R.U.C. headquarters ten minutes later, without even thirty pieces of silver. Once the words fall out of my mouth, Braithwaite no longer needs me. He is on the phone to the P.M., the Taioseach, and half the United

Kingdom. I can almost see the wheels of the military machine spinning behind Braithwaite's eyes. When I get up and leave, there is no fanfare, no "thank you very much, we'll be in touch," nothing.

The rain has slowed, and now it is just a kiss of cold wetness against my cheeks. I walk down the street toward the bus station. It isn't like I can go home, after all. I can't face those haunting eyes of the madman, my husband, though I do not even know for certain if he remembers what passed between me and God. He might be just as much a pawn as I in all of this. Except, of course, he's on the winning team.

The rain-darkened sidewalks glitter in the street light. Salt hangs in the breeze. Above, perched on a brick wall, a crow bobs its head and laughs at me. I pass an open window; inside I can see the neon-blue flicker of a television and two shadow forms huddling together on a sofa. The clouds are breaking. Here and there, I can see pinpricks of light, stars in heaven. It is turning into a beautiful night.

I take in a deep breath, the first real one I've had all evening, and make a decision. I'm not ever going back to that brick house on the Bogside or to the man whose eyes penetrate me, burn me. No, I have an old friend in Dumcree who will take me in, no questions asked.

The bus station is nearly deserted. The usual gaggle of unwashed, pot-smoking foreign boys huddle against the wall, probably having arrived too late to get a room in the youth hostel. The place smells of piss, and my heels stick wetly in places on the smooth concrete floor. After buying a ticket at the counter, I find a seat on a cold, plastic bench. Above me, a florescent bulb buzzes and snaps, sending a nauseating flicker of light onto my knit skirt.

A whisper of a breeze comes in from a broken window, and tickles my eardrums: *If you had not plowed with my heifer ye had not found out my riddle.*

"Sorry?" I turn, looking for the source of the noise. I expect to see a drunk mumbling to himself, but there is no one. Glancing over at the boys, I wonder if I could have overheard one of them, but they all face the walls, asleep in their ratty bags.

Now shall I be more blameless than the Philistines, though I do them a displeasure.

I jump, doing a half-slide on my seat.

I've heard voices before. Oh, most certainly, I might be mad, but I think everyone does at one time or another. The static on the radio or the trickle of water through a radiator transforms into a flock of people all talking at once. Our minds struggle to make sense of nonsense, and so we take order where there is none. But, this voice is different. This sound is distinct and clear; I understand every word. Though I wait patiently, it does not reveal itself as the hum of a heating vent.

I hug myself on the bench, clutching my purse tightly to my breasts.

Who hath done this?

The voice is so loud now, that it sounds as though it's coming from the overhead speakers. The boys in the corner, however, remain asleep.

I stand up on shaky knees and walk over to the ticket booth. The man behind the counter is balding, and in the traditional way, he's combed a few long strands of the remaining hair over his pate. He wears a polyester tie and an equally stiff looking shirt. I ask him, "Did you announce something?"

The man looks up from the leather-covered book he is reading and regards me. In the harsh light, his eyes reflect light, like a cat's.

"If you had not plowed with my heifer..." His voice is measured, even, and completely without county accent. I have heard this voice before.

I back away slowly, keeping my eyes on the man behind the counter. He stares beatifically. His eyes glow silver, and his face takes on a strange smoothness, as if it is slowly being recast in porcelain. Finally, I can't take it any more, and turning away, I break into a run.

My heels click loudly in the nearly empty bus station. Crashing through the swinging doors, I burst outside. The cool evening breeze hits my face like a slap, and I stop to catch my breath. The darkness comforts me, along with the smell of the pavement after rain - familiar, normal. In a few minutes, I convince myself I just imagined the voices. Passing cars hiss on the rain-drenched streets. I reach out a hand to flag down a taxi.

Headlights pass, but eventually an old-fashioned black taxi stops. The door swings open, and I step gingerly over the puddle in the gutter to sit primly in the back seat. The inside of the cab smells musty and faintly of old cigarette smoke.

I pull the door shut firmly, and say, "Take me to Dumcree Manor." I give the address of my father's estate; I'm going home.

"That's a long way out," the cabby says, looking back as if to check to see if I can afford the ride.

"I know," I say, showing him the wad of cash I stuffed into my purse before leaving Morrison's house. I carry a lot of 'mad money' since my life with Morrison is unpredictable.

Satisfied, the driver turns his attention to the road. I watch the streets of Londonderry roll past. Soon, we leave the city behind for country roads. My heart pounds less frantically in my chest and I think that, perhaps, I am finally free.

My eyes register movement along the side of the road. Though the clouds have broken, the moonlight makes eerie, ghostly shadows out of the branches of trees. I am not sure, at first, if what moves just ahead of us is man or animal. I decide it must be a hitchhiker, possibly one of the braver foreign boys from the bus station.

As the taxi passes the figure, I see his pale face. Our eyes meet through the streaked glass of the window, and I feel the old burn of Morrison's dark glance. I blink, and the figure dissipates into the shadows of the forest, and is gone.

"Leave me alone," I whisper, but I doubt God listens to me. Did he listen to Judas or any of those he set up to take the fall? Even his only son was willing to believe him so capricious as to forsake him in the final hour.

There are no answers to my question and I'm exhausted. I press the side of my head against the cool glass window. The put-put of the engine and the bumps along the street lull me to sleep. As my consciousness fades, I wonder fleetingly if I can ever truly hide from God's watchful eye or the long arm of His vengeance.

***

Fields of wheat are ablaze. Olive trees are consumed by fire. Howls of wounded animals assault the night air; the cries are so pitiful they sound like the wails of frightened babies. Morrison stands in the center of the blaze, though the fire doesn't dare to touch him. Instead, it licks at his heels like a supplicant.

In one fist, Morrison holds a squirming mass of fur and blood. It takes me a moment to realize he holds living foxes by their tails. In their panic, they tear and claw at each other. With the other hand, he sets their tails on fire. With a laugh, he lets them loose to run, howling, through the countryside. In his eyes I can see the fire...a fire that leaps out to grab me. I can feel its hotness on my skin, the sharp burn, then, the acrid smell of burning hair and flesh. I scream.

He says: *"Now I shall be more blameless than the Philistines shall, though I do them displeasure."*

I wake up with a start in my childhood bed, the smell of smoke still curling around my nostrils. I rub my nose to banish it, but it lingers like an unwanted guest.

A month has passed since I left Morrison. I did not expect him to try to find me, and he did not disappoint me in his disinterest. In fact, yesterday the news reported that he has taken up with a whore, some woman crazy about his hair. This, after he handed over the cache of arms, weapons he stole from a British barracks in order to make good on his promise. It seems I have gained nothing by my betrayal. I am still so little to him that he doesn't even seek retribution.

A shout comes from the courtyard. A cheer of a crowd follows it. I sit up, yawning. Isn't it a bit early for polo?

I get dressed slowly. The sun warms my cheek and pools in my lap. Despite the nightmare, I feel refreshed. Of course, I smile, rubbing the sheets of the bed and smelling sex; that might be because after so long I have finally found a man who touches me, who treats me as something more than furniture. A bore, the Windsor might be, but he is a kind man. I have had my fill of cruel rogues.

The cries come again. Jumping into slacks, I can no longer resists the urge to see what the noise is about. I pull the curtains all the way open and my heart stops. Men are standing in the courtyard. Each has a can of gasoline, and the man standing in the middle of them on a soapbox holds a lighter.

They are speaking, and though the voices should be garbled, I hear something of how Morrison wreaked his revenge after all, how he found out about my lover and, in a 'jealous rage', bombed an English village.

I push the window open with shaking palms. The voices that come to me are measured, singsong.

"Who hath done this?"

"Samson, the son in law of the Timnite, because he had taken his wife, and given her to his companion."

"No," I whisper, "Just leave me alone."

But, I know my plea falls on deaf ears yet again. Though His own hand sealed my fate, I am God's enemy.

Touching flame to gasoline, they set the house on fire.

Swallowed!
By Stephen M. Wilson

...I shall never sleep calmly again when I think of the horrors that lurk ceaselessly behind life in time and space, and of those unhallowed blasphemies from elder stars which dream beneath the sea...

"The Call of Cthulhu"
H. P. Lovecraft

<u>Chapter IV</u>

He wakes to the sound of gentle surf and the warm morning sun beating down on his almost bare back. Brushing his long, lank hair from his face, he opens his eyes and sees that he is laying facedown on an alabaster beach. He slowly raises himself to a sitting position to take in his surroundings. The beach stretches on for several leagues in either direction and on the far inland horizon, he can see the roof tops of a recognizable city. He had tried so hard to avoid this epicurean place, this poison city of madness, and as fate would have it, here he was on its charnel shore.

He turns his gaze seaward. His jaw drops at what he sees. Lying several yards away, half in the surf and half on the beach, is a grotesque malignancy of fantastic nightmare. The monstrosity is the size of a temple and has gulls picking at its green gelatinous flesh; flesh that is covered with parasites. Its anthropoid outline is simultaneously an octopus, a dragon and a human caricature with a tentacled head surmounted on a grotesque and scaly body - sprouting rudimentary wings. The beast looks like a creature that could only have crawled from the thighs of his own mother.

Within the mass of pulpy feelers, its massive mouth is ajar all dripping with green ooze and sinister with latent horror. A steaming path of gore putrid with the carcasses of decaying fish and other less describable things oozes from that cavern right to where he sprawls. The very sun of heaven seemed distorted when viewed past the polarizing miasma welling out from the sea-soaked perversion. Then memory hits him like a torrent and the last small vestiges of sanity finally leave him.

Later in the afternoon, villagers begin to gather on the beach to gape at the leviathan.

They have come to revel in the spectacle of your misery, taunts a familiar voice.

Yet the spectators avoid contact with the sallow bedraggled man who wanders amongst them; maybe it is the fetid smell of vomit and rot that wafts from his body or maybe it is his physical deformities, the twitching third arm barely covered by strips of filthy cloth that dangles from the middle of his chest and the crimson scrotum that is swollen to the size of a pomegranate; whatever the reason, they turn away when he approaches. He is unaware that he looks nothing like the handsome, statuesque man who had started this journey only weeks earlier.

He wanders away from the crowd and toward the city that awaits him - towards his destiny.

For over a month, a month of strange days, he wanders the streets of the city raving in delirium.

The end is near, you filthy, diseased heathens, the vile voice insinuates from within.

"The end is near, you filthy, diseased heathens!" The man repeats, at the top of his lungs.

He notices a queerness about the people of the city, whose predominant color is a grayish-green, though they

110

had white bellies. They were mostly shiny and slippery, but the ridges of their backs were scaly. Their forms vaguely suggested the anthropoid; while their heads were the heads of fish, with prodigious bulging eyes that never closed. At the sides of their necks were palpitating gills, and their long paws were webbed. They hopped irregularly, sometimes on two legs and sometimes on four; their baying voices croaking and jabbering in some hateful guttural patois.

One night he wanders into a dark alley and almost trips over the spread legs of a whore, who sits in the shadows on a mound of ash. She looks up at the man and grins, exposing diseased gums where teeth once hung.

"Honey for my honey," she cackles.

She is in a state of filth that rivals his own; topless, with small breasts that resemble shriveled figs. Her skirt is hiked up around her waist, and with both hands she morbidly and spasmodically claws in epileptic madness at her sex like a mongoose digging in the earth for snakes.

"Manna, for that *special* hunger," she moans luridly while spreading her outer labia to expose the moist interior of her body; offering it up to the man. She cackles again.

He starts to make his retreat from the alley, uninterested in the offer. One last comment from the harlot follows him.

"Come to mother."

Suddenly something snaps and an old familiar rage boils up inside forcing him to turn back towards the filthy whore.

"That's it, sweetheart; all yours," she croons.

For a brief moment, he sees not the Jezebel, but instead the creamy skin of his mother.

He approaches her.

"That's it my darling," she whispers through crimson lips, "You know how to please mommy." She winks at him and is once more the harlot.

He bends over her and embraces her head with his two normal hands, turning it upwards to face him. She closes her eyes and licks the pus from her scabby lips in expectation. He then swiftly shoves the fist of his third arm up into the waiting maw of her ravenous vulva. It is swallowed all the way to the elbow. She gasps and her eyes fly open.

"Oh, you like it rough," she murmurs. "Give it to momma rough. Come on."

He opens the fist that is buried inside of the woman's dank cave and grabs onto something that feels like a nest of sleeping snakes. His three arms work in unison and in one swift motion; he breaks the whore's neck and withdraws his arm from her wetness, his fist filled with her steaming still pulsating entrails.

Fleas, lice, and all other manner of parasites exit the dying body, avoiding the sizzling blood and acrid urine that spews from her dehiscent cunt, making way for new insects that will soon take their place and make the corpse their home.

He covers her with a piece of nearby tattered sackcloth and walks away.

Another day dawns.

It is time to leave this place, the voice orders him and he turns from her, making his way out of the city to a queer dark precipitous hill a few leagues to its east.

There is no vegetation of any kind on that broad expanse, but only a fine gray dust of ash which no wind seems ever to blow about. The trees near it are sickly and stunted, and many dead trunks stand or lay rotting.

112

There, under the instructions of the voice, he spends the morning gathering the dead branches with which he builds himself a rough shanty that faces the city. Then, like a true eremite, he plants himself in its shade and spends the remainder of the afternoon begging the voice to leave him alone; let him die.

At dusk, he lies down and falls asleep. When he awakes he notices that, overnight, a *kikayon* has grown from one of the dead branches at the top of his shabby booth. He eats the gourd, which is filled with bitterness and sickness, even the smallest bite inducing disgust. But he knows that it is poison and death will be a boon. He grays and turns brittle then perishes in the night. Within days, he is crawling with worms.

Chapter III

The tempestuous sea swallows him swiftly with its whirling and churning - its weeds wrapping around his calves and wrists and head, pulling him down into its abysmal darkness. He sees bizarre and disturbing objects in the surging water. A smile passes across his face as he starts to lose consciousness because, for once, the voice is quiet.

Thank you, he thinks, and then everything goes black.

As he slowly regains consciousness, the first sensation that he becomes aware of is a slushy nastiness as of a cloven sunfish, a stench as of a thousand open graves. In his childhood, back before the voice had come to rule his life, he had come upon a leper on the side of the road while returning from Joppa with a pot of fresh water.

The man had been curled up in a fetal position wearing only a filthy scrap of cloth around his mid-section. The rest of his naked, exposed body had been covered in scabrous, oozing sores. The boy had stood there a moment,

113

staring at the gaunt man in horrified fascination, wondering if he was dead or alive. He had then set down the clay pot and had snapped a twig off of a nearby bush to prod the bundle of diseased bones. When he had gotten within a foot of the leper and started to poke him, a small sound had escaped what was left of his lips. Thinking the man had spoken, the boy had leaned closer - mere inches - to the man's mouth to better hear what he was saying. Suddenly a loud belch had escaped the depths of the man's gut and erupted right into his face. He had jerked away, but not in time to escape the stench of rot and death that assaulted him. He had thrown up violently and ran home, the pot of water forgotten. In hindsight, he had figured out that the leper had been dead and what had happened that day was no more than the natural gas of decomposition.

The odor he now wakes to is something like that, yet much worse, mixed with the stench of rotting fish and just as he did on that long ago day, he retches several times; bringing up hot, chunky bile and seawater. This purging session goes on for several moments until he is finally reduced to dry heaves. Then the realization strikes him that he is in complete darkness.

He begins moving his fingers along the surface where his aching body lies. What they encounter make no sense to him. Every surface that he touches feels hot, wet and fleshy and there is a broad impression of vast angles, the geometry abnormal and loathsome, something redolent of spheres and dimensions apart from ours. It pulsates beneath his touch as if alive.

He sits up and starts groping the dark space in front of him, leaning to the left and then the right, his hand once again encounters the fleshy surface - a wall of it. He drags his hand tentatively along the bumpy, pulsating wall

114

Swallowed! by Stephen M. Wilson

dumbfounded. Then he begins to cry, for recollection is returning; he had been thrown into the raging sea. He remembers. Then he realizes that he must be dead and this, his hell.

How long the hot tears chased each other down his dirty face; it could have been minutes or days. What finally dries them is the revelation that for once he is alone, truly alone; ever since he had been tossed overboard, the voice has been silent. With this solace, he curls up into a little ball and falls asleep, a sleep wrought with nightmarish memories.

He is seven years old. He wakes from a peaceful sleep. It is the middle of the night. He wanders the house trying to discern the origin of the noise. He stops and listens. He hears it again, a faint, drawn-out moan. It is coming from his mother's room. He walks in that direction. He peeks into the room. His mother is naked and straddling a man who lies on his back. The man's eyes are closed in ecstasy. His mother, who is bouncing ecstatically up and down on the prone man, turns to him. She grins. She licks her crimson lips and winks. He watches as the man tightens his grip on his mother's hips and begins to convulse. A long moan of pleasure escapes his lips. It is his last, for the boy's mother leans forward and rips the man's throat out with her teeth. The dream shifts. He is five. He is playing in the back of the house. He falls asleep beneath a great olive tree west of the hut near the black swamp.

A noise wakes him. He opens his eyes and sees his mother throw something into the stagnant water. She looks around but does not see him, and makes her way back toward the small hut. He walks over to the pond. His mother had told him numerous times to stay away from it, that it is dangerous but he is bested by curiosity. He stands

115

at the edge of the moonlit waters, gazing into its murky depths. They were alive with a teeming horde of swimming shapes, the bobbing heads and flailing arms were alien and aberrant in a way scarcely to be expressed or consciously formulated. He hears a most detestably sticky noise as of some fiendish and unclean species of suction when, suddenly, a creature breaks the surface from below like a crab with pyramided fleshy rings or knots of thick, ropy stuff covered with feelers where a man's head should be, and wraps its tentacles around the boy's neck. He is half-dragged, half-sucked down into the unnamable abyss of the squalid, stagnant black mire.

The next thing that he remembers is his mother screaming at him as she slaps him across the face, "I told you to stay away from the water!"

He pulls away from her.

"I'm sorry, honey," she breathes, "Come to Mommy."

He walks timidly towards her and she pulls him to her breast, stroking his wet, slimy head.

He feels comforted by the words, the warm embrace, and her womanly scent.

"You know I love you the most," she croons. She puts her hands to the sides of his head and tilts his face upwards. Looking into his eyes she says "I love you" once more.

"What's this?" she asks as she notices that he is becoming erect.

Embarrassed, he tries to pull away from her embrace.

"It's okay, honey," she breathes in his ear, "Totally natural. My boy is becoming a man." She says this almost as if with pride. Then a cloud glazes her eyes. He knows the look, has seen it many time in the eyes of the older boys before one of the 'games'.

"Come," she urges. She grasps his hand and drags him toward her bedroom.

Later that night, he tries to make sense of everything as he cries himself to sleep.

The man wakes with the dream bringing a question to his mind.

"Who are you really?" he asks aloud.

An image flashes in his mind. Two fetuses entwined head-to-toe within each other's embrace. A pink sea surrounds them as they suckle on each other's penises.

I Am the Thing of the Idols. I Am the green, sticky spawn of the stars, the voice returns, *We...are one!*

The image changes as one of the twins begins to devour the other, the pink sea quickly turning red.

I am ravenous, my brother!

The man is stunned but knows the revelation to be true.

He had eaten his own brother! Even *in utero*, he had been a cannibal.

From this point on, he tries to ignore the fiendish buzzing, the incessant whispering of the hateful and unhuman voice as it continuously assaults him.

He languishes in the fleshy hell - the lonely, dark cell, so lonely that it could destroy the strongest of minds; the voice has infected his mind like a parasite, the only thing keeping him company. He knows that no one will ever understand what has brought him to this point. The voice is stronger and more pervasive then ever, and like his twin, the man is ravenous.

To sustain himself, he begins to gnaw on the walls of his prison. For the next few weeks - weeks that feel to him more like years - he eats, sleeps, and goes mad.

<u>Chapter II</u>

Wake up! It is time.

As his eyes open, he feels his body being jerked to and fro. He is slammed into the wall of his cabin, and then thrown out of his cot and onto the hard, planked floor.

Soon. Soon! The voice whispers luridly in his mind. *He will be here in moments.*

Realizing that a storm is raging, the man pushes himself into a sitting position, then stands and makes his way the few feet to the small portal above the table. It is being pelted with rain and hail. He opens it.

Beyond the portal, the squall has grown in strength and transformed into a tempest-a force that knew the secrets of a man's heart and could tear his soul to shreds. The rage of the storm mirrors that which twists and writhes like a hungry worm in his mind.

There is a knock on his door.

Dinner has arrived.

"Please go away," the man begs of the voice. "Leave me alone. Please!"

Do not be a coward! Open the door and let him in, it is time.

He opens the door, and there stands the beautiful young man, a plate of steaming food in one hand, a small clay jar in the other and a wicked grin on his face.

He enters the cabin, and walks over to the small table. The man closes the door behind the boy and turns to watch as he sets the two items down, and then turns, and without a uttering a word, drops his tunic to the floor.

A gift from the violent onslaught, the boy is like a beautiful, grotesque cherub.

His naked skin glows in the light of the oil lamp, his sandy blond hair tousled, his chest, muscular for his age with brown, coin-shaped nipples, his uncircumcised penis already half-hard and pointing right at him, his scrotum soft and smooth, making a mockery of the man's own deformed testicles.

No one deserves to be so beautiful, the voice taunts, *make him pay. You know how.*

He thinks of all that his suffering has caused him to lose - his innocence, his home, his sanity. All that remains is the voice and its determination to destroy him.

He grabs handfuls of the boy's fair hair, and pulls the ethereal face towards his own waiting mouth. His engorged tongue parts the boy's lips without resistance; it snakes into the pliant mouth, brushing across the smooth teeth, seeking out the warm pink tongue within. He then slowly retracts his own swollen tongue, enticing the smaller one of the boy to venture into his waiting maw. His teeth settle lightly, teasingly around the small pink muscle. His third arm slithers from beneath his robe.

The boy, his eyes shut, moans with desire and starts to gyrate against the hand, which wraps itself around his erect member and begins to stroke. As he gets more involved in the kiss, he reaches up and puts his small smooth hands over the older man's rough ones, which are still entangled in his hair. A moment goes by before he realizes that something is off. He lowers one of his hands to investigate what is going on at his crotch. He raises the hand again to explore the other two hands, which writhe and twist in his hair. He drops both hands and wedges them, palms out, against the man's chest. He tries to push away

119

from the man. The teeth tighten on his tongue. The speed and urgency of the strokes increase and become rough. He realizes the he is trapped in the sinister embrace.

Do it! The voice urges, *Make him pay like all the others!*

He tries to drown it out, but it is of no use; the blood has abandoned his brain to collect in his erect tongue.

As the boy begins to ejaculate, the man simultaneously rips the tongue from his pubescent mouth, swallowing it, and tears his spurting member from its scrotum. The boy convulses; then goes slack in his strong grip. He gently lays the beautiful body, now spurting blood and oozing ichor, onto the hard wooden planks and climbs atop him. He begins to feed.

After gorging himself, he falls asleep.

When a sailor later finds the mutilated body of the cabin boy with the bloodied man snoring beside him, hot bile erupts from his churning gut leaving a burning trail up the pathways of his chest and throat. The acrid vomit explodes from his mouth, splattering his own sandaled-feet as well as the mutilated body of the dead cabin boy; melting and mingling with the pool of tacky, already congealing blood. The sound of his retching causes the man to roll over in his sleep, exposing his third arm, which flops down and lands in a pile of offal in the center of the carnage. Its clenched fist still grips a globule that looks suspiciously like a boy's penis. This new revelation invokes fresh vomiting from the sailor before he turns and runs from the cabin.

Several minutes later, he returns with a dozen men. The madman is sitting on the floor with his back propped against his cot. His third arm is feeding him the boy's cock.

They drag him to the outer deck and in a few moments one of them returns with Ol' Cap'n Obed.

Even in his crazed state, the man sees that something is off about the captain. He is naked except for a strange diadem on his narrow head. The surface of his body appears as if its peeling from some cutaneous disease. His watery blue eyes bulge; never to blink. Through long fat lips, he begins to mumble an incantation without nouns, but only verbs and pronouns. As he continues, the sailors strip off their clothing and join the chant.

Ol' Cap'n Obed's rambling voice scrapes and whispers on:

"Ph'nglui mglw'nafh Cthulhu R'lyeh wgah'nagl fhtagn!"

Then, with large heavily veined hands, he brings a flute to his thick drooping lips and begins to play demonic music.

As he plays, the naked sailors encircle him, becoming a flopping horde; mindless amorphous dancers. They lift the maniacal cannibal and throw him overboard into the mighty eddying and foaming of the brine.

Chapter I

He expected it would be a perilous journey yet still he heads for Tarshish refusing the order. By rebelling against the voice, he is desperately trying to hold on to the last shreds of his sanity.

As he boards the Philistine cargo boat, the gray wood planks - brittle under his sandaled feet - look like the skeletal remains of a beached whale. He notices the intricate hieroglyphics carved into the hull of the *Alert* - aquatic symbols such as fish, eels, octopi, crustations, mollusks, whales and the like; and certain sort of men, damnably human in general outline despite webbed hands and feet, shockingly wide and flabby lips, glassy bulging eyes - and other features less tasteful. He recognizes the depiction of Dagon, the Philistine fish god.

Burly men load freight onto the ship and pay him no notice. He does catch the eye of an epicene cabin boy who smiles and walks toward him.

"You look lost," he says, "Do you need help?"

"I'm not sure where I am supposed to go from here, where my cabin is." He shows the boy his pass.

"Looks like we will be neighbors," the boy replies, taking the man's satchel, "Follow me, I'll show you."

As they make their way into the belly of the ship, he studies the boy's graceful movements of the boy and arousal stirs within his mouth.

Yes, the voice intimates, *Beautiful.*

"Go away!" He curses beneath his breath.

"I'm sorry?" the boy glances over his shoulder at the strange, attractive man.

"Nothing," he replies, "I just have a painful cramp in my thigh."

"Oh," the boy says, his full lips stretching into a smile. "Here it is."

They arrive at a rough heavy door which the boy opens exposing a utilitarian cabin, bare except for a squat table, a chair, and a threadbare cot. Over the table a small mold-covered portal looks onto a sky that is just beginning to cloud over. He sets the man's bag on the bed.

"If you need anything, I am two doors down, on the right. Most of the mariners say that I have magic fingers; I could come back later and work that cramp for you," he states. To the man's surprise, the boy winks at him.

"Thank you. I think I will take you up on that. I need to get some rest first."

Swallowed! by Stephen M. Wilson

"I'll come back in two hours with some dinner, and some tallow to rub into your thigh." He smiles at the man and exits the cabin, closing the door behind him.

Perfect! The voice speaks up, when they are finally alone. *That was too easy.*

He curls up and drifts into a fitful sleep. The boy has triggered memories of his childhood, images that shift in and out of focus. He dreams.

The voice had started when he was twelve. He went to bed one evening smooth and had woken up the next morning with soft, downy hair under his arms (even the small, wing-like, third arm had this new growth) and around his groin. While exploring the short, wiry pubic hair, he had also found that what used to be a loose piece of skin beneath his penis was now heavy, swollen, and dangling. He stroked the bulging sack and squeezed it lightly discovering something that felt like a large olive. Intrigued by this find, he had prodded a little further counting three more of these 'olives'. He knew what this meant. He had often played Adam & Eve with some of the older boys from the nearby town of Joppa, and these boys' testicles had already dropped. What confused him was the fact that he had four of them where his playmates had always had only two.

Later, that same afternoon, the voice had come. He was playing Samson and Delilah with an older boy named Nephi. Because he was younger and a 'freak', he had always played the female in these games.

After a few minutes of the familiar groping, Nephi had noticed the change in his playmate's organs.

"What's this?" he asked, cupping the younger boy's bulging scrotum, "Looks like it's time for a new game. Get down on your knees, Delilah, and put it in your mouth.

123

Move up and down on it." While giving these instructions, Nephi had reached up and untied the leather strip that held his hair into place, letting it fall loosely around his shoulders.

"Don't worry," he said, "when my seed comes, just swallow it. Put it into your mind that you are swallowing a bunch of tiny fish. It'll be easy."

The boy, 'Delilah', following orders, dropped to his knees.

Nephi spread his tunic and withdrew a rather large red erection.

"Come on now; show Samson that you love him," Nephi had said, putting his hands on the back of the younger boy's head and guiding his mouth towards the rigid member.

From the boy's position on the ground, Nephi's penis had been at eye-level and looked like an angry red cobra ready to strike.

After a moment of hesitation, the boy had gripped Nephi's waist, and pulling him forward, had wrapped his mouth around the pulsating flesh. It squirmed around in his mouth, probing for his tonsils. Within moments, Nephi began to convulse and applied pressure with his hands, shoving the mouth all the way to the base of his engorged penis, gagging the boy. Thick, venomous liquid had exploded into his strained throat.

At the moment of Nephi's orgasm, two unexpected things had simultaneously happened. While his two normal hands still gripped Nephi's waist, Jonah's third arm, which had always hung limp and lifeless from his chest, twitched, then shot up between the legs of the older boy, his clenched fist entering Nephi's rectum, the force pushing the older boy's cock further into his throat.

124

Second, a voice, seemingly from nowhere and everywhere all at once, spoke.

Bite it. Rip it from its root.

He had not known the origin of the voice, but instinct had taken over. At Nephi's severed member had slid down his semen-lubricated throat, it caused a gusher of a different kind; blood erupted into his upturned face. Nephi screamed, then slovered and gibbered before dying. After removing the extra appendage from Nephi's ass, the boy had licked it clean of blood and feces. Then climbed atop his molester and started ripping hunks of hair from his head with his teeth.

"Samson, I have found the secret of thy strength," he mumbled, his mouth full of bloody scalp.

Later on the same long ago afternoon, he had cleaned up the mess and dragged Nephi's body to the swamp for his daemon siblings to feast on. Even at that young age, he had grasped the irony, for it had been Nephi who had first taunted him with lurid stories about his mother and her offspring. Some had called her Black Widow, others a vampire. The grotesque tales had been shadowy and marvelous; of which grandmothers had whispered to children through the centuries.

His mother was a legend.

That same evening, he had started to have second thoughts about the existence of the voice; thinking maybe he was going mad. Much had been happening; he had felt confused and violated. Maybe it had been nothing more than rage. Still, he was curious. He had decided to probe the question.

"Are you there?" he had asked the empty room around him.

"Hello? Who are you?"

She Nailed a Stake Through His Head

I AM, a booming voice answered. He jumped. The voice had not been external, but somehow remained *separate* from his own thoughts. He had heard the stories of Moses and *his* experience with an unbodied voice - and Noah and Avraham and Yosef and Samuel.

"Who ... who's th ... there?" he had asked again.

I AM!

Again the voice. Then wicked laughter.

It told him that he was to go to Nineveh.

That dream drifts away and merges into a new one:

A naked woman lies on her back. Her stomach is swollen and covered in a fine sweat. She is screeching like an owl as she strains in childbirth. The woman is his mother. To her right stands a man. He knows the man as Amittai, his father. It dawns on him this dream is a memory of his own birth.

She pushes one last time, a scream escaping her throat. The babe is shoved into the world with a gush of warm blood and afterbirth; a third arm protruding from his gore-slick alabaster chest; a small broken wing.

Lilith brushes her sweaty hair from her brow, lifting the infant to her waiting mouth, and uses her teeth to sever the cord that connects them. Swallowing it, she puts the infant to her breast.

"My little dove," she whispers, "I will call you Jonah."

Amittai's adam's apple bobs up and down, as he swallows nervously. Lilith turns to him and smiles. She then bares her sharp teeth and rips his throat out.

Dedicated to Chuck Palahniuk

Last Respects
By D.K. Thompson

I pulled the sharpened dentures from my mouth and dropped them in the cup of water. Crimson strings threaded from the incisors through the liquid. The bed creaked as I lay back; the taste of blood still lingering on my tongue. It had been a long night and even vampires get tired, especially ones my age.

I looked at the picture of Jesus nailed to the wall. He stared down at me with a sad smile and I felt my wife's cold impression on the bed. Moments like these were the hardest, forcing the truth; she was dead. Even with her funeral the next day, I couldn't believe she was gone.

Downstairs, my grandchildren stomped and crashed about, giggling and ignoring their parents' admonishments. They had arrived earlier that night for Catherine's funeral. Children are great but grandchildren are better. I don't have to get up in the middle of the night and their parents pick up after them. It's a joy to see them grow, learn to walk, speak and eat. There's a pleasure in their faces at meal time that most of us older folk have forgotten.

Us older folk.

It's humorous to hear the stories our ancestors told about our adversaries before the war: *we* are immortal and will never die. But you, *you* will not last and will leave no trace of your existence. You will be forgotten because your lives are not only unmemorable, but insignificant. These are the fears of every people and culture so what could be more terrifying than an enemy who cannot be destroyed, as we claimed to be. But they were only stories. No one lived forever, certainly not us.

I've read stories about the sorrows immortals suffered because of how much they had seen over their long lives. What rubbish. I would trade my mortality for their immortality in a heartbeat if it meant another day with Catherine.

A scream rang out from downstairs. I smiled when I heard applause; my grandchildren being praised by their mother as the scream faded to a whimper and the giggles were replaced by slurping sounds.

***

"You spoil them too much," my daughter Molly told me the next evening, less than an hour after dusk. She stood over the stove, frying up the leftovers from the last night. There was a large pail next to her, filled with body parts, waiting to be tossed onto the griddle. The aroma of garlic filled the room and I felt my mouth watering.

"I just wanted them to have a good time and get some exercise, Molly," I told her. "Get their natural instincts flowing. Kelly especially looks a little pale. She could use a bit more blood in her veins. But I didn't clean up after them."

Molly grunted, flipping the meat with her spatula. Thankfully, she'd inherited her mother's cooking skills. "They're too young to move the bodies themselves. I had to drag the carcasses in here before I went to bed so I could cook them up first thing this evening."

"What?" I asked, over-doing my incredulousness enough to cause Molly to crack a smile. "Did my parents ever pick up after me when I made a mess eating? I think not. I had to both catch my dinner and clean up after myself.

That's the problem with kids today; not enough independence."

"It's just we try to keep the children in a routine. We want them to be strong and fend for themselves. And Patrick and I never give them seconds."

I bent down and kissed Molly's forehead. "How can I refuse my grandchildren's wishes? Permit an old man some pleasure, my dear. Where is Patrick, anyway?"

Molly sighed. "Kel and Jamie started bouncing on our bed before sunset. Patrick took them out for a walk around the farm while I slept a little more."

"That was very kind of him."

"Yes. He's very kind," she said. "Sometimes I think maybe too kind. Papa, I need to ask you something. Did you ever wonder if you made a mistake? If you shouldn't have married Mama?"

"Is something wrong between you and Patrick?"

"No, not exactly. We're fine, I guess. But he feels so far away from me sometimes, like he's isolating himself."

"He's not isolating himself right now," I said.

"Not from the kids, at least," Molly replied. "Sometimes, he talks to me about things I don't understand, wants things I don't know how to give him and doesn't want what I can."

I crossed my arms. "Do I really want to hear about this kind of problem from my daughter?"

Molly laughed. "No, not that kind of thing, Papa. I don't know, maybe it's nothing."

"Maybe. Have you talked to him about it?"

"Better. I fight with him about it."

"Ah."

"Did you and Mama ever fight?"

"No, not really. Not for a very long time, at least. We were very happy, your mother and I." I remembered how hard it'd been on Catherine to move out to the farm but eventually she got used to it. And after being married for forty-seven years, it hadn't seemed like there was anything new or worthwhile to fight about.

"So what is it Patrick does or doesn't want?"

She poked the meat in the frying pan and let out a sigh. "All of this," she said, gesturing around the house. "Anything about me, about us."

I shook my head. "Molly, what are you talking about?"

Just then the door opened, and Kelly and Jamie rushed inside, hugging my legs. "Grandpa, Grandpa," Kelly shouted. She was dressed in overalls and her hair had been braided into pigtails, much like her mother's had been at that age. "We saw all the animals out in the barn. Can we have another? Please?"

Patrick walked in after them, pulling off his mittens, his thin face white from the cold. He shook his head and I could see his cheeks flushing red.

"You already asked your father, didn't you?" I asked.

Jamie's freckled face went red when our eyes met and he thrust his hands in his pockets, and looked at the floor. Kelly watched me, waiting.

"What did he say?"

"That we had to wait until tonight," said Kelly. She stuck out her bottom lip, hoping I'd spoil her still.

"Well, then you'll have to wait until tonight, my sweethearts. I'm sure there will be plenty for us all."

Patrick smiled and mouthed, "Thank you."

Molly scooped some of the leftovers from the frying pan onto a plate. Kelly grabbed one of the leg bones and started gnawing on it, but Jamie just shook his head. "I told you it wouldn't work," he hissed at Kelly as they marched up the stairs.

"Why did you give them those?" Patrick asked Molly. "It'll spoil their appetites."

"It's only a snack," Molly replied. "Dinner's a long way off. They'll be fine."

Patrick muttered something and walked out of the room. Molly never stopped to look at him, just kept poking the meat with her spatula.

Feeling awkward, I walked to the door and put on my old hat, the one with the ear muffs my grandfather had worn during the war. "I better go see to the livestock and make sure your little monsters didn't scare them too badly."

"I'll come with you," Molly said.

I remembered how much fun she had helping me when she was a little girl, how Catherine had tied up her thick blonde hair into pigtails. The top of her head couldn't touch my waist. Now she was only a head shorter than me and her pigtails were gone, her hair cut at her shoulders in a very contemporary fashion. Was it really that long ago? Did time move by so fast?

"How can I say no to my little girl?" I asked and a smile lit up her face. "Just make sure you bundle up. It's cold out tonight."

***

Howls from the livestock filled the night air. The snow had started to fall, covering the grass with a thin blanket. Our boots crunched through the snow, echoing

131

across the field. The pale light of the full moon lit up the field as we walked back to the old barn, the red paint peeling off its wooden planks. Our breath floated before us in the chilled air, lingering like apparitions reluctant to disperse. Part of me was thankful for the cold. It helped bury the stench of human waste that usually permeated the farm.

The animals whimpered and cowered away from the door as I opened up the pen.

I have a movie in my head of Molly helping me in the barn as a little girl, dressed in overalls and just a little older than her own children. She would carry a pail that splashed water with every step she took and put it in the livestock's troughs. She always had such a calming effect on the animals out in the barn.

For parents, such memories are sometimes only figments of the imagination. The way they want to remember their children often replaces the reality.

Such was not the case with Molly. If anything, her movements were more graceful, attaining even more trust with the animals.

All those years ago, I had always worried she would spook one of them, that they'd strike out at her. I am not ashamed to say that even that night I tensed at the thought – so many of them towered over my Molly when they stood up straight (though they rarely did that anymore). What could be more terrifying than something horrible happening to your child? It's in the nature of parents to protect. And I had already lost so much in the last week.

"Be careful, dear," I told her when one of them growled and backed away. "They're not used to you."

"It's okay, Papa. I'm fine."

Molly didn't seem to notice my fear and her confidence actually seemed to relax the animals. They backed away from her at first but she talked to them, holding out her hands so they could sniff and touch her with their own, and realize she meant them no harm. Eventually, they let her close enough to ruffle their hair and beards or massage their backs (they always loved that) or even hug them as she had when she was a little girl. She had never been squeamish about the livestock's fate, even back then. It was a fact of life to her. A benefit of growing up on the farm, I suppose.

"I forgot how peaceful it is out here," Molly said. "How quiet it can get."

"You always did like the country," I said. "Your mother and I didn't think you'd take to the city like you have."

"How are you doing, Papa?"

"Tired. I am always so tired."

"But how are you *doing*?"

I realized then what she was asking, why she had come out to the barn with me.

"I'm fine, Molly. It's sweet of you to worry but you don't need to. Really. I..." My throat ached and I had to swallow and take a deep breath before I continued. "Most of the time I don't even realize she's gone."

I tossed out some of the leftovers Molly had prepared, fried meat, some that still resembled arms and legs. The blood had all been drained, of course. The livestock had no taste for it. They pushed and shoved and dove down in the straw and dirt to capture their food.

"Do we need to move some of them over to the church?" Molly asked.

"I already did last night, before you and Patrick and the kids arrived. I wanted to make the most of our time together."

She gave me a hug.

"Are you sure you can afford it, Papa?"

"It's the least I can do for your mother's funeral," I told her.

***

The church was only just up the street. By the time we got there, the sanctuary was already half-full but the first row had been reserved for us. I sat down beside Molly; my grandchildren squirmed between her and Patrick, uncomfortable in their Sunday clothes.

Jesus hung on a crucifix at the front of the church. Strange that our adversaries used to shove the image of our God into our faces, thinking He would save them instead of us. They did not understand that the God they worshipped was ours, not theirs.

The preacher shook my hand and said how he was sorry for my loss. He was a handsome young man, always smiling. Even that night, he had a small smile on his face. I did not tell him that Catherine had never appreciated his sermons. Instead, I said, "Thank you."

After everyone sat down, the preacher handed me a dish filled with tiny strips of fried meat. Catherine had wanted her funeral begin with communion.

"The last night with his disciples, Christ feasted with his friends," said the preacher. "He passed food to them and said, 'This is my body which has been broken for you. Eat it in remembrance of me.'"

I put the piece of flesh inside my mouth. It was tough and difficult to swallow. The church bought from an overstock warehouse; not from my crop.

I tried to focus on the symbolism of the act instead of politics. Jesus had shed His blood for our sins and asked us to drink it so we would one day be resurrected just as He was. But all I could think of was Catherine, how much I missed her and wondering why she had to leave so soon.

The preacher continued, "After the meal that same night, Christ passed a cup around to his disciples and said, 'This is my blood which has been shed for you. Drink it, in remembrance of me.'"

The blood tasted metallic on my tongue but went down much easier than the flesh.

"I am the resurrection and the life. No man comes to the father but through me."

Was the road to heaven that narrow? Was there a heaven at all? I wondered. Was this just another myth our ancestors created? But looking at Catherine's casket and Christ hanging on the cross over her, I started to wonder if even gods die. I didn't know, but I hoped that wasn't the case. I wanted to see Catherine again, filled with life. Not like the last time I'd seen her in the bathtub, wrinkled and spent; her tongue hanging out of her mouth - her eyes empty.

I didn't hear the rest of the preacher's sermon. Usually I found them enlightening but maybe Catherine had been right about him after all. Easier on the eyes than on the ears. She'd had a way of judging character, even though I'd often been blind to her observations.

After the preacher finished, friends and strangers approached to hug me or shake my hand, offering condolences after viewing the body.

Patrick and Molly kept a tight grip on the children, telling them not to look, worried what it might do to them psychologically, but most of all wanting them to remember their grandmother as she'd been when she was alive, not the artificial way she'd been displayed in the casket. It had been my idea to leave the casket open during the service. Old-fashioned, I guess. Catherine had always said I was a traditionalist. But when they finally closed the lid, I was thankful.

Patrick helped carry the casket out into the fading night before dawn arrived. They put it down in the fresh white snow, re-opened the lid, and trudged back toward the church.

A funeral is an all day affair, starting very late in the night. The departed is prayed for and set outside, awaiting the sun to lay it to rest. Instead of sleeping, we stay up to commiserate, mourn, and stare out of the tinted windows into the beautiful, forbidden light. Then the body is gone; the casket remains as empty as Christ's tomb.

But dawn did not come, at least not right away. Dark clouds had rolled over the plains, blocking the daylight. A storm was on its way. A part of me felt relieved. I wasn't ready to let go of her. I felt something nagging at me, something I needed to understand first.

Snow started to fall. The animals I'd brought over the previous night began to bray and cry out, their moans echoing throughout the sanctuary. At least today that custom would be satisfied.

Then, for a few seconds, the clouds broke and the sun cut through the sky. In the empty field, Catherine's body caught fire inside the casket.

I cried out, realizing I would never see her again. Not in this life, at least. She was gone. There was so much I still wanted to tell her, so much I wanted to share. I just wanted her to hear me say "I love you" one more time.

The clouds soon returned, hiding the ground from the sun but the flames continued to flicker above the casket, their warm orange tongues licking at the gray sky. Plumes of smoke curled above the field. The surrounding snow began to melt from the heat and the casket sank a little into the newly created mud.

Jamie started to sob, burying his head in his mother's knee, but Kelly just stared out into the field; her eyes wide and her mouth opened. Molly clutched them both to her and I felt her body sink against mine. Patrick watched, standing apart from his family, his face strained.

After the flames died down, the preacher spoke up. "The family has provided a meal downstairs in the basement and requests that you join them. It's important that in this hour, we be with the family of our dear sister and show them our love and support."

The animals were shivering in their chains downstairs, waiting. We selected our dinners and the animals were moved to the tables and forced to lie down. They writhed in their chains and whimpered as we took our seats beside them, stroking them gently to calm them and then lifting their limbs to our lips. Some of the livestock screamed when bitten. Others soon got over the initial shock and became, not less excited, but seemed to take pleasure from it, as if they understood the price their sacrifice paid for us and found peace with it.

Molly and the children had already started eating, blood staining their faces. Patrick sat with his head bowed, probably still blessing the food.

Poor bastards, I thought as I looked into the eyes of the female strapped to our table. I wonder if they feel as we do?

Then I chuckled to myself, appreciating the ridiculous questions we find ourselves grappling with in grief. I tore into her flesh and her warm blood filled my mouth.

The food did not comfort me. I don't even remember hearing the woman as I drank from her veins, whether or not she screamed and kicked or moaned.

The day finally ended. The guests had eaten most of the livestock but not all. Patrick agreed to take the leftovers back with him when he and Molly and the kids returned to the farm. The children had fallen asleep before dusk and I knew he and Molly must have been tired. But I wasn't ready to go home yet.

"Are you going to be okay?" Molly asked me. "It's so cold outside."

"I just need some time alone," I told her. "I'll walk home." I pulled her aside, away from Patrick and her children. "You didn't get to tell me last night. What is it that Patrick wants?"

"Oh, it's nothing, Papa. I shouldn't have said anything to you about it. It was selfish and horrible timing."

"Please."

She stared at me, a confused look on her face. "You know how thin he is, how pale he looks? When we first started dating he never ate a lot. I didn't think much about it then." Her voice trailed off and she shrugged. "He doesn't like eating the livestock, Papa. He doesn't think it's right. He says that they aren't really animals and he should eat other things instead."

I shook my head, remembering how I thought Patrick had been praying before dinner. "Other things? What other things?"

Molly sighed. "Other kinds of livestock. Cows. Pigs. Anything else."

"Pig blood?" The idea disgusted me. "He wants my daughter and grandchildren to drink pigs' blood?"

"No, not all of us. Just him."

"Just him?" I repeated. My thoughts drifted to Catherine, everything she'd wanted that I hadn't given her, that I had refused to give her. Her misery when she'd first moved to the farm. All the things I hadn't understood, that had gone unsaid. I thought she'd change but she was stubborn and I thought she wanted to change me. But I couldn't change anymore than she could.

I'd never understood, I realized. Why is that only now, when she's gone, I finally understand?

"Papa?" Molly asked. "What's wrong?"

"I'm sorry, Molly. I don't know what to tell you."

Molly kissed me on the cheek. "I didn't expect you to."

"I love you, my Molly," I said, hugging her to me.

"I love you, Papa. Come home soon."

I watched them go before I walked out to the field, saw Patrick open the door for Molly and lift the kids into the backseat of the pick-up truck without waking them. I waved as they pulled away, and then walked into the field.

The casket would be gone before the night ended but nobody would have moved it yet. I'm not sure what I wanted to see or do when I got out there. Certainly not fall down in the snow and cry like a child, but that's exactly what I did as I looked inside the casket, empty but for the ashes.

"There's so much I didn't tell you," I sobbed. "So much I didn't understand."

The moon hung above me where the sun had been hours before. I spent the next few hours sobbing and praying, trying to make up for past mistakes and regrets. I talked and talked and talked; hoping for some kind of answer or sign from God that my prayers weren't in vain, that there would be a resurrection, that I would see Catherine again. But all I heard was the howl of animals from my farm, their cries surrounding me, filling the field, empty except for me.

I stayed out there beside her empty casket, waiting.

Author Bios

Christi Krug's speculative fiction has appeared in *Defenestration* and *The Absent Willow Review.* Her poetry, nonfiction and short stories have appeared in *Umbrella, qarrtsiluni, Halfway Down the Stairs, Colored Chalk* and *VoiceCatcher.* She coaches beginning writers at Clark College and independently through http://christikrug.blogspot.com. Horror closest to home: she torments her family with weird healthy recipes.

Daniel Kaysen's short dark fiction has appeared online at *Chizine* and *Strange Horizons* and several times in the print magazine *Black Static.* His short story "The Rising River" was reprinted in Ellen Datlow's first *Best Horror of the Year* anthology. He lives in the south of England.

Gerri Leen lives in Northern Virginia and originally hails from Seattle. She came to fiction writing late in life and writes stories in many genres, including fantasy - both light and dark, and often centered around mythology - science fiction, and literary. Look for her upcoming collection of short stories, *Life Without Crows,* in early 2010. She also dabbles in poetry and has several poems published. You can find her stories in such places as: *Sword and Sorceress XXIII, Return to Luna, Triangulation: Dark Glass, Footprints, Sails & Sorcery, Origins, Desolate Places,* and *GlassFire.* Visit http://www.gerrileen.com to see what else she's been up to.

She Nailed a Stake Through His Head

Elissa Malcohn was a 1985 John W. Campbell Award finalist and is on the recommended reading list in *The Year's Best Science Fiction, 26th Annual Edition*. Her work appears in *Asimov's*, Hugo Award-winner *Electric Velocipede*, Bram Stoker Award-winner *Unspeakable Horror*, IPPY Silver Medalist *Riffing on Strings*, and elsewhere. When not writing she enjoys photographing bugs, singing, performing spoken word at open mics and deconstructing scripture with her Midrash buddy Michael Koran. She lives in central Florida with her partner Mary C. Russell. More info, plus free downloads of her Deviations series, may be found at http://home.earthlink.net/~emalcohn/index.html.

Lyda Morehouse is a big fan of God and the author of the AngeLINK tetrology. The well-recieved series is religious cyberpunk mash-up which includes Archangel Protocol and Apocalypse Array, which won the Shamus and Philip K. Dick (2nd place) awards respectively. A prequel to the series called Resurrection Code is forthcoming from Mad Norwegian Press in December of 2010.

Lyda leads a secret life as the psuedonym Tate Hallaway, a best-selling romance writer. Tate will have two books this year: *Honeymoon of the Dead* (the last in the Garnet Lacey series) coming out from Berkley May, and *Almost to Die For* (the first in the vampire princess of Saint Paul series) from NAL in August. She lives in Saint Paul, Minnesota with her partner, six year old son, four cats, two gerbils and countless fish. You can find her all over the web, most directly at http://www.lydamorehouse.com

Romie Stott is an editor of the slipstream magazine *Reflection's Edge*. Her work has been published by *Strange Horizons*, *Jerseyworks*, *The Huffington Post*, and *Death List Five*, among others. As a filmmaker (working under the name Romie Faienza), she has displayed work at the National Gallery in London and the Dallas Museum of Art, and participated in Jonathan Lethem's Promiscuous Materials Project. She is a founding member of the film and art collective Rocker Box Gasket.

D.K. Thompson is a devout member of the church of Fox Mulder, whom he describes as the 13th apostle of Christ (screw Chris Rock). He is a recovering Baptist and practicing Quaker. He likes exploring his faith through his fiction and has written stories about Saint Darwin, Puritan Noir, God-Shaped Boxes and serial killer saints who get swallowed by alien spaceship whales (although he's still trying to find a home for that last one). His work has been published by Pseudopod, Apex Online, Murky Depths, Hub, and Variant Frequencies. He lives with his wife, two children, and two cats in Southern California, where he can be found wandering through bookstores with a glassy-eyed expression in search of coffee and interesting things to read. He is planning on launching a podcast on geeks and faith in late 2009. Break blog and drink coffee-flavored Kool-Aid with him at http://krylyr.livejournal.com

Catherynne Valente is one of the most exciting voices in modern fantasy. She has written poems, novels and short stories including *Palimpsest* (Random House 2008), *The Girl Who Circumnavigated Fairyland in a Ship of Her Own Making* (available online) and *A Guide to Folktales in Fragile Dialects* (Norilana Books 2008). She has won numerous awards and her blog is at http://yuki-onna.livejournal.com.

Stephen M. Wilson is Poetry Editor for *Doorways Magazine*, editor of *microcosms* and co editor of several issues of the Dwarf Stars Award anthology. His own writing has appeared in such places as *The Queer Collection, Avant-Garde for the New Millennium, The Vault of Punk Horror, The Huffington Post, Star*Line, rattlesnake review, Tule Review* and *Space and Time Magazine*. He received an honorable mention from Ellen Datlow in the *YBFH* series as well as several Rhysling Award nominations. Stephen has three teenagers and lives in California.
More at: http://speceditor666.livejournal.com

CPSIA information can be obtained at www.ICGtesting.com
Printed in the USA
BVOW011345190612

293091BV00004B/3/P

9 780976 654674